ABUNDANT LIVING

Who You Are in Christ

SIGNATURE SERIES

NewLife
PUBLICATIONS

Abundant Living: Who You Are in Christ

Published by
New*Life* Publications
A ministry of Campus Crusade for Christ
375 Highway 74 South, Suite A
Peachtree City, GA 30269

Design and production by Genesis Group

Printed in the United States of America

Unless otherwise indicated, Scripture quotations are from the *New Living Translation*, © 1996 by Tyndale House Publishers, Inc., Wheaton, Illinois.

Scripture quotations designated NIV are from the *New International Version*, © 1973, 1978, 1984 by the International Bible Society. Published by Zondervan Bible Publishers, Grand Rapids, Michigan.

Scripture quotations designated TLB are from *The Living Bible*, © 1971 by Tyndale House Publishers, Wheaton, Illinois.

Scripture quotations designated NKJ are from the *New King James* version, © 1979, 1980, 1982 by Thomas Nelson Inc., Publishers, Nashville, Tennessee.

Scripture quotations designated KJV are from the *King James Version*.

CONTENTS

This book, part of the Bill Bright *Signature
Series*, is a condensation of *Living
Supernaturally in Christ*, which
was published in 2000.

As Members of

Global Founding Partners

the following families are helping to fulfill
the Great Commission through helping to
train Millions of Pastors around the world.

Bill and Christie Heavener and Family
Ed and Edye Haddock and Family
Stuart and Debbie Sue Irby and Family

FOREWORD

OVER 35 YEARS AGO, as a student at the University of Arkansas, the spiritual lights were going on in my heart. The love of God had already begun to sink in, turning my cold heart into a white-hot flame for Jesus Christ. In God's providence, my path crossed that of a CCC staff member and my life would never be the same. I thank God that Bill Bright recognized the potential of college students to influence their world for Jesus Christ.

That same year my wife, Barbara, found herself in a small group with a Crusade staff woman. She thought she was a Christian, but soon placed her faith in Christ and began to see her life change.

We spent three months as summer staff at Arrowhead Springs, and during that time I grew a "spiritual foot." As Bill Bright spoke, I learned to walk with Christ in the power of the Holy Spirit. It was a life-changing summer. I would never see my campus, or my world, through the same set of eyes.

Bill Bright's faith and his vision to reach the world were an overflow of the abundant life he had discovered in Christ. We just sensed that Bill had directions from God and we felt confident to follow.

Looking back, I realize that it took a great deal of faith to allow me to lead the Family Ministry for the world's largest non-denominational Protestant missionary organization. I will be forever grateful that Bill expressed his belief in God and in me that God would someday use us to impact millions.

Throughout my thirty-plus years with Crusade, Bill has modeled what it looks like to be a bond slave of Jesus Christ, and constantly reminded me that our God is not small.

The power of the Holy Spirit is too frequently measured by what has been done rather than by what can be done. As you read this book, if you know anything about Bill Bright, you will recognize his complete faith in the Spirit of God to empower anyone to do great exploits.

May you be encouraged to explore who you are in Christ so that you may truly experience the abundant life He came to give.

DENNIS RAINEY

INTRODUCTION

YOU DESIRE TO know God better. No doubt this is one reason you are reading this book. It is written for Christians. If you have placed your trust in the Lord Jesus Christ to forgive your sins and give you eternal life, you are in a place of highest privilege. When you consider your routine of work, bills, and day-to-day struggles, do you have difficulty feeling privileged? Perhaps you see celebrities smiling from the television screen and think how fortunate they are. Yet, as a Christian, you have value and significance beyond anything this world can offer. And if you fully understand the riches of God's glory in this life and the next, you will never be the same.

If you love Jesus Christ and give your life to Him, God assures you in His Word that you will obtain the immeasurable riches of an inheritance in heaven and a supernatural life on earth. In 1 John 5:12, you are promised, "Whoever has God's Son has life; whoever does not have His Son does not have life." As a believer in Jesus, God's Son, you can experience an intimate relationship with your heavenly Father and have meaning, purpose, and a life of supernatural victory.

Are you missing out on the kind of life God wants you to have? It is impossible to live the Christian life through self-effort. But you can experience a supernatural, abundant life by faith as you allow the risen Son of God to live through you. As you explore the wonderful truths of God's Word in this book, you can learn to live beyond your circumstances and limitations.

Before proceeding, take a moment to tell God how much you appreciate Him. Thank Him for saving you and for making you a new creation in Christ. Ask that His Holy Spirit will open your spiritual eyes so you may see, understand, and utilize the resources and blessings He has given you in His Son. Finally, tell Him how excited you are about the intimate relationship you have with Him now and for the rest of eternity.

Begin your day with a prayer, surrendering and dedicating your life to the lordship of Christ. Ask Jesus to think with your mind, speak with your lips, and love others through you.

one

UNDERSTANDING YOUR
SPIRITUAL BLESSINGS

*How we praise God, the Father of our
Lord Jesus Christ, who has blessed us with
every spiritual blessing in the heavenly
realms because we belong to Christ.*

EPHESIANS 1:3

HOW WOULD YOUR life be different if you were
adopted by the most powerful, virtuous, wealthy
person in the world? How would your self-image
change because your father was so prestigious?
How would you feel about this person who lav-
ished you with such favor?

The adoption offer has been made, but not
by some world-famous human. The Creator and
Sovereign Ruler of the universe has chosen you
to be His dearly loved child!

God's Word gives us this wonderful promise,
"When the right time came, God sent His Son,
born of a woman, subject to the law. God sent Him
to buy freedom for us who were slaves to the law,
so that He could adopt us as His very own chil-

ABUNDANT LIVING

dren. And because you Gentiles have become His
children, God has sent the Spirit of His Son into
your hearts, and now you can call God your dear
Father. Now you are no longer a slave but God's
own child. And since you are His child, everything
He has belongs to you" (Galatians 4:4–7).

One night, a house caught on fire. It was the
home of an orphaned boy and his grandmother. As
the flames quickly spread throughout the house,
the boy was trapped upstairs. His grandmother attempted to rescue him, but she died in the flames.
Fortunately, a man who saw the fire heard the
boy's cries. He climbed up an iron drainpipe to the
lad's window. With the boy clinging to his neck
and a firm grip on the drainpipe, he carefully lowered himself and the boy to safety.

A few weeks later, a public hearing was held
to determine who should have custody of the boy.
A teacher, a farmer, and the town's wealthiest citi-
zen all gave reasons why they should be chosen to
give the boy a home. But the sad boy only stared
at the floor.

Then a stranger walked to the front of the
room and announced his desire to adopt the boy.
He slipped his hands out of his pockets and held
them up for the crowd to see. His palms bore hid-

eous scars. The boy cried out in recognition and leaped into the man's arms. This was the man who had saved the child's life! His hands had been seared when he climbed the hot iron pipe. As the boy nestled in his savior's arms, the other men walked away. Those marred hands had settled the issue.[1]

In the same way, the Savior's nail-pierced hands have settled the issue for you. The Lord's sacrifice saved you and made you a child of God. Jesus described those who believe in Him as "children of God raised up to new life" (Luke 20:36).

As a believer, you are not an orphan who is homeless. You have an incredible parent—a loving Father who cares for you and provides for you each moment of every day. And you have a marvelous home waiting in eternity. Even now, you can experience peace, joy, and a sense of belonging through your Father's Spirit—the Holy Spirit —who has made your heart His home. You are very important to God because you are His dearly loved child.

Free to Soar in Christ

Does your life reflect your noble heritage as a child of the Sovereign Ruler of the universe?

11

A story is told of a baby eagle that fell out of its nest and was found by a farmer who raised it with his chickens. The eagle watched the chickens peck at their food and began to live as they did, never attempting to fly.

One day, a naturalist passed by the barnyard and wondered why the king of the birds was confined with chickens. He longed to free this magnificent bird from such a limited existence, so he attempted to teach it to fly. At first, the bird would only run around the barnyard flapping its wings.

Many of us do not fully understand who we are in Christ, and do not experience the blessings God has for us.

Finally, the naturalist took the bird to a high mountain and lifted it toward heaven. "You are an eagle," he told the bird. "You belong to the sky. Stretch forth your wings and fly."

The eagle began to tremble. Finally, it spread its wings and, with a triumphant cry, soared into the sky.

In the following weeks and months, this eagle may have flown over its old barnyard and even remembered the chickens with nostalgia. But it never returned to live like a chicken.[2]

Like the eagle, many of us do not fully understand who we are in Christ. As a result, we do not experience the incredible blessings God has intended for us. Instead, we must see ourselves as our loving Father sees us. Listen to how much He loves us:

> *Long ago, even before He made the world, God loved us and chose us in Christ to be holy and without fault in His eyes. His plan has always been to adopt us into His family by bringing us to Himself through Jesus Christ. And this gave Him great pleasure (Ephesians 1:4,5).*

God is not some distant architect of the universe who remains light-years away pondering His creation. He is a loving, involved Father who desires an intimate relationship with you. If you truly comprehend how much God loves you, your life will never be the same. He has an amazing plan for you both now and for eternity. Your self-worth will no longer be based on human success or status, but on the person you are in Him.

Because you are God's precious child, He has given you certain privileges which will be yours forever. The acrostic CHILD will help you remember that God...

C   *Conforms* you to Christ's character

H   *Hears* you when you pray
I   *Indwells* you with His Spirit
L   *Loves* you unconditionally
D   *Disciplines* you lovingly[3]

God Conforms You to Christ's Character

The Scriptures say, "Those God foreknew He also predestined to be conformed to the likeness of His Son, that He might be the firstborn among many brothers" (Romans 8:29, NIV).

At creation, God declared His marvelous plan for you. Genesis 1:26 reveals, "God said, 'Let us make man in our image, in our likeness'" (NIV). God intended human beings to reflect His character. What an amazing calling! But instead of being mirrors of their awesome Creator, Adam and Eve disobeyed God. The first humans' fall into sin distorted human nature so the mirror was cracked almost beyond repair. Jesus, however, mirrored God's character perfectly. In Him, human beings may have a new nature—His nature.

God knows you cannot become like Christ through your own abilities or in your own strength, so He lovingly and patiently shapes you, like an artist sculpting a masterpiece.

The great sculptor Michelangelo was chiseling a large block of stone when someone asked him how he created such beautiful statues. He answered, "The angel is caught inside the stone. I simply keep chipping away everything that isn't the angel."[4]

God is chipping away at your imperfections to release the beautiful creation He has birthed. The "sculpting" may be aided by difficult trials, gracious blessings, or inspiring Scripture.

God's Word commands, "Don't copy the behavior and customs of this world, but let God transform you into a new person by changing the way you think. Then you will know what God wants you to do, and you will know how good and pleasing and perfect His will really is" (Romans 12:2).

Our heavenly Father will do His part to conform you as you invite God to work in you. Paul assures us, "God is working in you, giving you the desire to obey him and the power to do what pleases him" (Philippians 2:13).

God Hears When You Pray

The Bible promises, "We can be confident that He will listen to us whenever we ask Him for anything in line with His will. And if we know He is listening when we make our requests, we can be sure that He will give us what we ask for" (1 John 5:14,15).

Day or night, God hears your every prayer. What a privilege! You have unlimited access to your almighty Creator God because you have placed your faith in His Son, Jesus Christ.

During the Civil War, a Union soldier who had lost his father and older brother in the war tried to gain an audience with President Abraham Lincoln. He wanted to ask the president for an exemption from military service so he could go home and help his mother and sister with spring planting. But he was told, "The president is a very busy man. Get back out there and fight the Rebs like a good soldier." Disheartened, he left and sat down on a park bench near the White House.

A small boy approached the soldier and asked why he was so sad. The soldier poured out his heart to the boy. Then the boy took the soldier by the hand and said, "Come with me." He led him into the White House, past the guards, the generals, and high-ranking government officials. Then they entered the office where President Lincoln was discussing battle plans with his Secretary of State! The soldier was mystified at how this boy could walk unhindered into the president's office. Then President Lincoln looked up and said to the boy, "What can I do for you, Todd?"

Todd replied, "Daddy, this soldier needs to talk to you." This boy was Lincoln's son!

The soldier pleaded his case and was exempted from military service.[5]

Jesus' death and resurrection demolished the barrier separating us from God. As God's dearly loved children, we can approach our heavenly Father with all our joys and sorrows. As a child crawls up into his daddy's lap, we too can climb into our Father's arms and tell Him all that is in our hearts. What an honor to have such an intimate relationship with our awesome Creator God and Father!

As you talk to your heavenly Father, remember that prayer also involves listening to Him. It is exciting for me when I stop during my prayer to ask, "Lord, do you have anything to say to me?" As I listen, He speaks to me.

God Indwells You with His Spirit

The Bible explains, "Because you are sons, God sent the Spirit of His Son into our hearts, the Spirit who calls out, 'Abba, Father'" (Galatians 4:6, NIV).

Your heavenly Father gave you the Holy Spirit as a seal of your relationship with Him. Ephesians 1:13,14 explains, "When you believed in Christ, He identified you as His own by giving you the Holy Spirit, whom He promised long ago. The Spirit is God's guarantee that He will give us everything He promised and that He has purchased us to be His own people."

You are so special to God that He permanently marked you as belonging to Him.

You are so special to God that He permanently marked you as belonging to Him. The Holy Spirit has been placed within you as proof of God's calling in your life. As the Holy Spirit resides within you, He teaches, guides, and equips. He will make the things of God known to you and will glorify Christ. In John 16, Jesus describes the Holy Spirit as your Counselor and the Spirit of truth. Jesus also promises that the Holy Spirit will be with you forever.

The Spirit even helps you pray. Paul writes, "The Holy Spirit helps us in our distress. For we don't even know what we should pray for, nor how we should pray. But the Holy Spirit prays for us with groanings that cannot be expressed in words. And the Father who knows all hearts knows what the Spirit is saying, for the Spirit pleads for us believers in harmony with God's own will" (Romans 8:26,27).

Often when you come before your loving Father in prayer, you do not really understand His will or your needs. You only know that you feel hurt or confused or dissatisfied with your situation and the world's solutions. The Holy Spirit knows God's will. He can penetrate your conscience, search your heart, and show you what is best. But you must make sure no sin gets in the way of the Holy Spirit working in your life. Yet, when you do sin, God provides a remedy. Through a process that I call "Spiritual Breathing," you can exhale the impure and inhale the pure.

Exhale—Confess
The Bible explains, "If we say we have no sin, we are only fooling ourselves and refusing to accept the truth. But if we confess our sins to Him, He is faithful and just to forgive us and to cleanse us from every wrong" (1 John 1:8,9).

Confession means that we agree with God concerning our sins. This involves at least four considerations:

1. Agree that your sin is wrong and grievous to God. Be sure to actually name specific sins.

2. Acknowledge that God has already forgiven you through Christ's death on the cross for your sins.

3. Demonstrate your repentance by a change in your attitude and behavior.

4. If you have wronged others, try to make things right.

Inhale—Appropriate by Faith

Now that you, through confession, have exhaled the sin that interrupted your relationship with God, inhale the fullness of the Holy Spirit by faith. Claim Ephesians 5:18 and ask the Spirit to fill you and control you. Then enjoy a renewed fellowship with your heavenly Father as you are controlled and empowered by His Spirit moment by moment. And remember, although your sin may grieve God and short-circuit the Spirit's power, it can never change God's love for you.

God Loves You Unconditionally

The Bible tells us, "See how very much our heavenly Father loves us, for He allows us to be called His children, and we really are!" (1 John 3:1).

God's love does not depend on what you do. It depends on who He is. The Bible's famous love chapter, 1 Corinthians 13, says, "Love never gives up, never loses faith, is always hopeful, and endures through every circumstance" (v. 7). This is God's love for you.

The story is told of a prince and his family who were captured by King Cyrus of Persia. The great monarch asked the prince, "What will you give me if I release you?"

The prince answered, "Half of my wealth."

"And if I release your children?"

"Everything I possess," the prince replied.

"And if I release your wife?"

"Your majesty, I will give myself."

King Cyrus, moved by the prince's devotion, released all of them. As the prince and his family were returning home, the prince commented to his wife, "Wasn't Cyrus a handsome man?"

"I didn't notice," his wife said with a smile. "I could only keep my eyes on you—the one who was willing to give himself for me."[6]

Your supreme God and Creator gave Himself for you. Jesus declares in John 15:13, "Greater love has no one than this, that he lay down his life for his friends" (NIV). God demonstrated His com-

mitment to you by taking on human form and dying for you. What love!

God Disciplines You Lovingly

The Bible tells us, "My child, don't ignore it when
the LORD disciplines you, and don't be discouraged when He corrects you. For the LORD corrects
those He loves, just as a father corrects a child in
whom he delights" (Proverbs 3:11,12).

Just like earthly children, God's children must
experience discipline. Discipline is necessary to
mature and grow in character. God lovingly disciplines you so you will become more mature in
your walk with Him.

God's discipline is for your good. The Bible
explains, "Our fathers disciplined us for a little
while as they thought best; but God disciplines us
for our good, that we may share in His holiness.
No discipline seems pleasant at the time, but painful. Later on, however, it produces a harvest of
righteousness and peace for those who have been
trained by it" (Hebrews 12:10,11, NIV).

Parents who care about their children will discipline them. Proverb 13:24 states, "If you refuse
to discipline your children, it proves you don't
love them; if you love your children, you will be

prompt to discipline them." I fell in love with our two sons, Zac and Brad, the first time I saw them. I love them even more today, although they are now mature adults. When they were young, I spanked them when they were disobedient. I am sure that I shed more tears while I was spanking them than they did. Each time I would explain that I disciplined them because I loved them. After I finished spanking them, I would ask, "Why did I spank you?"

They would reply, "Because you love me."

The only way children learn to control their emotions, share with others, treat people with respect, and speak politely is through discipline and example. Our heavenly Father provides both. God has given us the perfect example in Jesus.

Imagine a display case filled with junk. You have some lovely things you want to place inside, but first you must clean out the worthless items.

As Christians, we are God's display cases. He uses discipline to remove our sin and pride so He can fill us with His beauty. This process can be painful for the moment, but will be productive for eternity. The result will be peace, righteousness, and other fruit of the Spirit.

Our Father is the Ruler of the universe! How

thankful we should be for the wonderful privilege of being His children. As His offspring, we can enjoy His love, care, and commitment as we pursue intimacy with Him by faith.

God wants you, His dearly loved child, to be blessed by His incredible treasures!

ALLOWING CHRIST TO LIVE THROUGH YOU

I myself no longer live, but Christ lives in me. So I live my life in this earthly body by trusting in the Son of God, who loved me and gave Himself for me.

GALATIANS 2:20

YOU HAVEN'T really lived until..."

You often hear this phrase in ads or from people you know claiming that you have not truly experienced life until you have driven a particular car, vacationed in some exotic locale, or indulged in a certain delicious dessert.

But are these earthly pleasures really what produce true, meaningful life?

Jenny, a happy five-year-old with bouncy, blond curls, was waiting with her mother in the checkout line of a discount store when she saw a string of glistening white faux pearls in a pink foil box. "Oh please, Mommy," she asked, "can I have them? Please, Mommy, please?" Her mother glanced at the price and shook her head.

When Jenny got home, she dumped the contents of her piggy bank on her bed and counted out her pennies. That night, she did more than her share of chores. The next day, she picked dandelions for the neighbor for ten cents. Then on her birthday, Grandma gave her a new dollar bill. At last she had enough money to buy the necklace.

Jenny cherished her little fake pearls.

One night when her father finished a bedtime story, he asked Jenny, "Do you love me?"

"Oh yes, Daddy. You know I love you."

"Then give me your pearls."

"Oh, Daddy, not my pearls! You can have Princess—the white horse with the pink tail from my collection. Remember, Daddy? The one you gave me. She's my favorite."

"That's okay, honey. Daddy loves you. Good night." And he gently kissed her cheek.

Several nights later when her daddy came to pray with her, Jenny sat crumpled on her bed with her legs crossed. Her chin trembled and her face was wet with tears.

"What is it, Jenny? What's the matter?"

Jenny slowly lifted her small clenched fist to her daddy. She opened it. Inside was her pearl necklace. Her voice quivered as she said, "Here, Daddy. It's for you."

With tears in his own eyes, Jenny's daddy accepted the cherished dime-store necklace. Then he reached into his pocket, pulled out a blue velvet case, and gave it to her. Inside was a strand of genuine pearls. He had them all the time. He was just waiting for her to give up the imitation pearls so he could give her the genuine treasure.[1]

The genuine treasure God wants to give you is the supernatural life of Christ. What a tremendous adventure! Yet if you were to honestly examine your life, what would you discover? Are fake treasures robbing you of an abundant life in Jesus Christ? Does your heart desire a comfortable lifestyle carefully wrapped in a fancy box? Are you clutching in your hand a longing for the world's approval or for love at any cost?

Counterfeit riches will keep you from receiving the real treasure God has for you. God wants to fill your life to overflowing with His love, grace, and power. He holds this abundant life "in His pocket" eager to present it to you. How true is the inspired quote from the missionary and martyr Jim Elliot, "He is no fool who gives what he cannot keep to gain what he cannot lose."[2]

ABUNDANT LIVING

Our Lord Jesus declares in Mark 8:34,35, "If any of you wants to be My follower, you must put aside your selfish ambition, shoulder your cross, and follow Me. If you try to keep your life for yourself, you will lose it. But if you give up your life for My sake and for the sake of the Good News, you will find true life." *The Living Bible* states that only those who do the latter "will ever know what it means to really live."

In Galatians 2:20 Paul explains the secret to living supernaturally: "I have been crucified with Christ: and I myself no longer live, but Christ lives in me. And the *real* life I now have within this body is a result of my trusting in the Son of God, who loved me and gave Himself for me" (TLB).

Paul gave up his life and all the world's false treasures for Jesus. He allowed Christ to live His life in and through him so completely that he could not "speak of anything except what Christ has accomplished through me" (Romans 15:18, NIV). As he let Christ renew his mind, he adopted God's perspective on the world. Everything Paul did, every day he lived, he did through faith by trusting in his living Savior. Paul describes this process in detail in the Book of Romans.

The following acrostic, CROSS, may help

you remember the five essential steps to living supernaturally in Christ:

C *Concentrate* on who you are as a new creation in Christ (Romans 6:3–5).

R *Regard* yourself as dead to sin and alive in Christ (Romans 6:6–11).

O *Offer* your body to God as an instrument of righteousness (Romans 6:12–15).

S *Surrender* your will continually to God (Romans 6:12–15).

S *Stay* dependent on Christ throughout the day (Romans 8:9–14).

Concentrate on Who You Are as a New Creation in Christ

God's Word promises, "Therefore, if anyone is in Christ, he is a new creation; the old has gone, the new has come!" (2 Corinthians 5:17, NKJ).

The first step to living in Christ is to simply recognize and accept the truth about who you are in Him. When you became a Christian, you became a new person. The core of who you are is no longer the same. All your sins—past, present, and future—are forgiven, and Christ has clothed you in His righteousness.

Paul says in 2 Corinthians 5:21, "God made Him who had no sin to be sin for us, so that in Him we might become the righteousness of God" (NIV).

Often a generous person is described as someone who will give the shirt off his back. Jesus gave us the righteousness off His back. Isaiah says, "When we proudly display our righteous deeds, we find they are but filthy rags" to God (Isaiah 64:6). But Jesus exchanged our rags for His righteousness—and we will be clothed in His righteous garments for all eternity.

One day a man toured a paper factory that makes the finest stationery in England. He asked, "From what is the delicate paper made?" He was shown a huge pile of old rags. He was told that the rag content is what determines the quality of the paper. The man would not believe that those dirty rags could be used for anything good.

Six weeks later he received a package of paper from the company with his initials embossed on it. On the first page were written the words, "Dirty Rags Transformed."[3]

The same is true of your life in Christ. God has taken your attempts at righteousness, which are filthy rags, and transformed them through the righteousness of Christ. Because you are now clothed in His righteousness, your sins are forgiven and you are justified—declared righteous! Your old nature no longer has power over you because you have a new identity and a blessed future.

Regard Yourself as Dead to Sin and Alive in Christ

Paul declares in Romans 6:11, "You should consider yourselves dead to sin and able to live for the glory of God through Christ Jesus."

Because of Christ's sacrifice, you are as dead to sin as a corpse is dead to this world. It cannot respond to any pleasure the world offers. No appealing aroma, glitzy picture, or sultry music can cause that dead body to get up and indulge. In the same way, you are to consider yourself dead to the desires and attractions of sin.

Yet we walk around in flawed, finite bodies that want to do wrong. In God's eyes we are dead to sin, but each day we have to consciously submit ourselves to the control of the Holy Spirit and decide to live according to how God sees us—according to our new nature. Paul writes, "I advise you to live according to your new life in the Holy Spirit. Then you won't be doing what your sinful nature craves. The old sinful nature loves to do evil, which is just opposite from what the Holy Spirit wants. And the Spirit gives us desires that are opposite from what the sinful nature desires. These two forces are constantly fighting each other, and your choices are never free from this conflict" (Galatians 5:16,17).

On a cold day, a man stood on the edge of Niagara Falls and watched birds swoop down to snatch a drink from the water. As the birds dipped down for a drink, tiny droplets of ice formed on their wings. As they returned time after time for additional drinks, more ice weighed down their bodies until, finally, they could not rise above the cascading waters. Flapping their wings, the birds suddenly dropped over the falls.[4]

This is how sin affects our lives. Some sins may seem small, but they are like those tiny droplets of ice. Each time you choose to follow your old habits of sin, you are saying "no" to the new life Christ has given you, and, like those birds carried over the edge of Niagara Falls, you may pay dearly.

Colossians 3:3 explains, "You died when Christ died, and your real life is hidden with Christ in God." Christ redeemed you and gave you eternal

life that begins *now*. You have the indwelling
Holy Spirit enabling you to withstand temptation.
Consider yourself a new creature instead of a sin-
ner, for sin has no power over you. Remember,
you are dead to sin and alive in Christ!

Offer Your Body to God as an Instrument of Righteousness

Paul urges, "Do not let any part of your body become a tool of wickedness, to be used for sinning.
Instead, give yourselves completely to God since
you have been given new life. And use your whole
body as a tool to do what is right for the glory of
God" (Romans 6:13).

The human body can be used for terrible evil
or great good. Compare Adolph Hitler with Mother
Teresa. Or rock singer Jim Morrison of The Doors,
who destroyed his body in his pursuit of pleasure,
and the martyr Jim Elliot, who offered his body
to accomplish a great good.

Paul urges us, "Dear brothers and sisters, I
plead with you to give your bodies to God. Let
them be a living and holy sacrifice—the kind He
will accept. When you think of what He has done
for you, is this too much to ask?" (Romans 12:1).

As I look back on my own experience of walking with the Lord for half a century, and as I have studied the Scriptures and observed the lives of thousands of believers, I have concluded that it is absolute folly for a Christian to live one split second out of the perfect will of God. If you realize how wonderfully great, holy, and righteous God is and what He has done, you can never be satisfied with living a mediocre Christian life. The privilege of knowing, loving, and serving the Lord is so awesome that to sacrifice this for any temporary pleasure—money, sex, power, fame—is ludicrous. Nothing compares to the abundant life of Christ living in and through you.

You have an amazing calling! As a Christian, you are to proudly display the cross of Christ. When you exchange the "treasures" of your former life for a cross, God will use you to win the greatest war of all—a spiritual one. He has a wonderful, perfect plan and, in His mercy, allows you to play an integral part if you will only consecrate yourself as an instrument of His righteousness.

Surrender Your Will Continually to God

Paul encourages us, "As slaves of Christ, do the will of God with all your heart" (Ephesians 6:6).

Before the fall of Satan, there was but one will

in the universe—God's. Dr. Donald Grey Barn-house explores this idea in his book *The Invisible War:* "The quality of eternity is the fact that there is but one will—the will of God. Then all was holy, all was righteous: there was no evil whatso-ever." But then a second will came into the uni-verse, "rising from the heart of Lucifer...In addi-tion to the voice of God, there was now a second voice saying: 'I will.'"[5]

We echo Satan's rebellion when we choose our own way instead of God's way, when we exert our will over God's will. Each time we claim our "rights" and fail to submit to the perfect will of our marvelous Creator and Savior, we cause dis-cord, pain, and guilt. The only means to bring peace and joy back into our lives and to this fall-en world is to crucify our will by surrendering our fleshly desires and our stubborn pride to the Lord. We must say as Jesus said to His Father, "Your will be done" (Matthew 26:42).

Jesus is the perfect example of one who sub-mitted His will to the Father. Although He Him-self was God, Jesus declared in John 6:38, "I have come down from heaven to do the will of God who sent Me, not to do what I want." How amaz-ing that Jesus surrendered all His rights and His personal ambitions to accomplish the will of His heavenly Father.

Surrendering ourselves to God will have far-reaching effects on our lives. In the RCA Building in New York City stands a gigantic statue of Atlas, who, with muscles straining, is holding the world on his shoulders. This powerfully built man can barely stand under his burden. On the other side of Fifth Avenue is Saint Patrick's Cathedral. Behind the high altar is a little shrine of the boy Jesus, perhaps eight or nine years old, holding the world in one hand.[6]

We must give all of our life to Him and ask Him to change our hearts so we will want to do what pleases Him.

How true this is for believers. When we hold onto our life and pursue our own desires, we are like Atlas, struggling under the weight of an unpredictable world. "Submission" is not a popular concept, but our ability to submit to God determines whether we struggle through life like Atlas or enjoy the blessings of entrusting our "world" to the all-powerful Creator of the universe.

Jesus submitted to the Father, even to the point of dying on the cross for our sins. We, too, must submit to Christ. We must give all of our life—our desires, needs, personal rights, and even our choices—to Him and ask Him to change our hearts so we will want to do what pleases Him.

Stay Dependent on Christ Throughout the Day

Scripture declares, "You are not controlled by your sinful nature. You are controlled by the Spirit if you have the Spirit of God living in you... For all who are led by the Spirit of God are children of God" (Romans 8:9,14).

Once you realize that you are a new creature and picture yourself dead to sin, you must offer your body, possessions, and will to God each day. But only with Christ's power can you "take up your cross" daily. Only Jesus can give you the ability to live the Christian life, so you must remain vitally connected to Him. He is the source of your spiritual nourishment.

In John 15:5, Jesus declares, "I am the vine; you are the branches. Those who remain in Me, and I in them, will produce much fruit. For apart from Me you can do nothing." But how do we "remain" in Christ so that we receive a constant flow of spiritual food?

Feed on God's Word. Paul tells Timothy, his son

in the faith, "All Scripture is inspired by God and is useful to teach us what is true and to make us realize what is wrong in our lives. It straightens us out and teaches us to do what is right. It is God's way of preparing us in every way, fully equipped for every good thing God wants us to do" (2 Timothy 3:16,17). The Bible is God's love letter to humans. The more we read it, the better we get to know Christ. And the better we know Him, the more we will trust Him. To know Him is to love Him and to love Him is to obey Him.

Pray. Prayer is communication with God. The Gospels are filled with accounts of Jesus praying to the Father. Paul tells us to "pray continually" (1 Thessalonians 5:17). This involves both talking to God and listening to what He has to say to us.

Be sensitive to the leading of the Holy Spirit. Jesus told His disciples, "When the Spirit of truth comes, He will guide you into all truth" (John 16:13). As you read the Bible and pray, listen for the Holy Spirit's gentle prodding through a verse you have read, a word spoken by a wise Christian, or an impression placed on your heart.

Confess your sins. Sin will short-circuit your communication with God. Scripture promises, "If we confess our sins to [God], He is faithful and just to forgive us and to cleanse us from every wrong" (1 John 1:9). You can receive God's forgiveness by confessing your sin—agreeing with God that it is sin—and by repenting—changing your attitude and behavior and making things right with those you have wronged. Then you can enjoy God's forgiveness and the fullness of the Holy Spirit.

Stay vitally connected to Christ's body. Scripture describes believers as a body with Christ as the head. Imagine a finger trying to function apart from its hand. Hebrews 10:25 tells us, "Let us not neglect our meeting together, as some people do, but encourage and warn each other, especially now that the day of His coming back again is drawing near."

Recognize who you are—a new and holy being, no longer dominated by sin, but consecrated for righteousness! And, by faith, surrender your will to God. Crucify your pride, your love for this world, and your need for people's approval. And in all these things, draw upon the life-giving sustenance of Christ. Then your loving Savior will powerfully live in and through you.

"You haven't really lived" until you live supernaturally as our loving Savior, Jesus Christ, makes possible. What an amazing adventure!

THRIVING IN GOD'S
SPIRITUAL FAMILY

*Now all of you together are Christ's body,
and each one of you is a separate and necessary part of it.*
1 CORINTHIANS 12:27

IN A RECENT POLL, 81 percent of Americans
agreed that "an individual should arrive at his or
her own religious belief independent of any
church or synagogue." In fact, one respondent
named Sheila stated, "I can't remember the last
time I went to church. But my faith in myself has
carried me a long way. It's 'Sheila-ism.' Just my
own little voice."[1]

Individualism and autonomy are two charac-
teristics cherished by most Americans and numerous cultures around the world. We pride ourselves on being independent and self-sufficient.
But is this how our loving Father wants us to live
out our faith? Previously we explored the wonderful blessings of being a child of God. But as

God's children, do you and I have a need for spiritual siblings or family? Does Jesus Christ want us to "go it on our own" or to belong to a community of believers?

Perhaps we can learn a lesson from one of God's most amazing creations.

Towering along California's northern coastline are the largest living things on earth—the majestic redwood trees. These mighty monarchs pierce the sky at heights of 300 feet and boast a circumference of more than 40 feet. The Grizzly Giant tree—the largest of the sequoias—is more than 2,500 years old. One would think that trees this large and ancient must have massive root systems that plunge hundreds of feet into the earth. However, a redwood's roots are actually quite shallow, lying barely below the soil. The secret to the sequoias' strength is that these majestic trees grow only in groves so each tree's roots can intertwine with the roots of the trees near it. When the strong winds blow, they hold each other up![2]

In a similar way, our wonderful God created us to need others. He did not intend for us to live in isolation, and He does not want us to live out our Christian faith alone.

Just as the cross has a vertical and a horizontal

piece, our identity in Christ has both a vertical and a horizontal aspect. As believers, we are related to God, but, like the mighty redwoods, we are also connected to each other. In 1 Corinthians 12:27, Paul explains, "All of you together are Christ's body, and each one of you is a separate and necessary part of it."

As members of the body of Christ, our identity has three dimensions:

- Each of us is *distinctive*. We have a unique and significant role to play in the body of Christ.

- Each of us is *dependent*. We need and are needed by the other members.

- Each of us must be *directed*. We must work together under orderly leadership for the good of the whole.

Christ's purpose for His body is to mature us as believers and to reach the world through us. We cannot accomplish these objectives alone. Only by working together in community can we be Christ's body—His hands and feet—ministering to the world He loves.

Let us look at six aspects of our identity as members of Christ's body. The acrostic MEMBER will help you remember that God…

M *Made* you part of His spiritual family

E *Equipped* you with spiritual gifts for ministry

M *Matched* you with specific needs in the body
of Christ

B *Baptized* you into one body for unity

E *Enlisted* you to build up others in Christ

R *Redeemed* you to love others[3]

God Made You Part of His Spiritual Family

The Bible tells us, "You Gentiles are no longer strangers and foreigners. You are citizens along with all of God's holy people. You are members of God's family" (Ephesians 2:19).

What an amazing privilege that God has chosen us to be part of His family!

Vonette and our sons are my immediate physical family. But I have a large extended family as well. The same is true spiritually of each of us.

Your immediate spiritual family is the local body of believers where you fellowship and worship. But you are also part of an extended family —the universal church—all believers everywhere for all time. No matter your nationality, race, gender, or denomination, we are *blood relatives*. We are related by the blood of Christ, which was shed for us when He died on the cross for our sins.

Our God knows that all believers need to be fed and encouraged by other Christians. One of the ways to maintain an intimate relationship with Christ is by staying vitally connected to the body of Christ. Imagine an ear sitting off by itself trying to hear. Equally ridiculous is the belief that we do not need to be part of a community of believers. Just as we need the love, support, and nurture of our physical family, we need the same from our spiritual family. This is where we can encourage each other, grow to maturity, learn family values, and discover our gifts.

Just as we need the love, support, and nurture of our physical family, we need the same from our spiritual family.

God Equipped You with Spiritual Gifts for Ministry

According to the Scriptures, "God has given gifts to each of you from His great variety of spiritual gifts. Manage them well so that God's generosity can flow through you" (1 Peter 4:10).

God has generously bestowed spiritual talents and abilities on each of us so that together we can fulfill the amazing plan God has for His church in this world and the next.

Paul explains, "He is the one who gave these gifts to the church: the apostles, the prophets, the evangelists, and the pastors and teachers. Their responsibility is to equip God's people to do His work and build up the church, the body of Christ" (Ephesians 4:11,12).

God is not concerned how our gifts compare to another believer's spiritual abilities. He cares about how well we use what He has given us. Jesus illustrates this truth in the parable of the talents. A man entrusted three servants with various talents or measures of money. One servant received five talents, another two, and a third servant one.

The first two servants doubled their talents and earned their master's approval. He was pleased because they had faithfully invested what they had been given. But the third servant buried his talent and did nothing with it. Consequently, his talent was taken away and given to the one who had ten talents (Matthew 25:14–30).

In evaluating your own giftedness, ask yourself: When I spend time with other Christians, what needs do I notice first? What tugs at my heart? This can be an indicator of your spiritual gifts. But be careful. Do not become so worried about discerning or using your spiritual gifts that you lose your willingness to serve. It is through service that your spiritual gifts are revealed and developed. And remember that the body of Christ needs the gifts and service of every member.

God Matched You with Specific Needs in the Body of Christ

The Scriptures explain our role in the church this way: "We will hold to the truth in love, becoming more and more in every way like Christ, who is the head of His body, the church. Under His direction, the whole body is fitted together perfectly. As each part does its own special work, it helps the other parts grow, so that the whole body is healthy and growing and full of love" (Ephesians 4:15,16).

Each believer has a vital part to play in Christ's body. The Bible explains, "In fact, some of the parts that seem weakest and least important are really the most necessary" (1 Corinthians 12:22).

In March 1981, President Reagan was shot.

We all recognize how important the president of our country is, especially in times of war or economic crisis. Yet while he was hospitalized for several weeks, the government went on. That event probably had no impact on your daily life.

However, several years later, the garbage collectors in Philadelphia went on strike. The city was a mess! Trash piled up until the rotting garbage became a health hazard. Philadelphians felt the impact of the garbage collectors' absence.

The president is highly esteemed and vitally important, yet even he is dependent on his garbage collector!

In a similar way, the roles in the family of God that are less visible are vitally needed to support the more visible work of pastors, teachers, and evangelists. Think back to the human body. We rarely pay any attention to our kidneys or liver, but if they malfunction, our skin and hair will show it and our whole body will eventually suffer. Instead of envying those with the most visible positions, we must faithfully develop and use the gifts we have to fulfill the unique purpose God has for each one of us.

God gave each of us gifts for a purpose. We must use our abilities and resources, or we will miss out on the blessings of service to our Master.

If our goal is God's glory, we will delight in the ministry He has given us. And we will work together in *unity*.

God Baptized You into One Body for Unity

The Bible declares, "Some of us are Jews, some are Gentiles, some are slaves, and some are free. But we have all been baptized into Christ's body by one Spirit, and we have all received the same Spirit" (1 Corinthians 12:13).

Our marvelous Creator does not want differences in personalities, backgrounds, worldly status, or spiritual gifts to create discord in the body of Christ. God wants His family to live in unity. Ephesians 4:3 challenges us, "Always keep yourselves united in the Holy Spirit, and bind yourselves together with peace."

We all have a particular role in God's divine economy, but we are not fulfilling that role unless we have a spirit of cooperation and partnership. The Bible explains it this way: "Just as our bodies have many parts and each part has a special function, so it is with Christ's body. We are all parts of His one body, and each of us has different work to do. And since we are all one body in Christ, we belong to each other, and each of us needs all the others" (Romans 12:4,5).

Modern medicine has only strengthened this biblical analogy. The human body is a marvel of "unity in diversity," beginning at the cellular level.

Each human body is a vast array of different cells all working together in concert. Malfunction of even a few cells soon affects nearby cells and may cause serious illness, such as cancer.

Because of the interdependence of its parts, the human body needs direction, which is the function of the brain. Likewise, Christ—the head of the church —directs His body. As each distinct member of Christ's body follows His direction, the spiritual family will be united in harmony.

The path to unity is humility, submission, and forgiveness.

The path to unity in the body is humility, submission, and forgiveness. Paul urges us, "Is there any encouragement from belonging to Christ? Any comfort from His love? Any fellowship together in the Spirit? Are your hearts tender and sympathetic? Then make me truly happy by agreeing wholeheartedly with each other, loving one another, and working together with one heart and purpose. Don't be selfish; don't live to make a good impression on others. Be humble, thinking of others as better than yourself" (Philippians 2:1–3).

If we are humble, we will have no problem submitting to those in the church whom God has placed in authority over us. Also, we will be willing to forfeit some of our own desires to meet the needs of other members of our spiritual family. This attitude of submission promotes unity.

Forgiveness is also essential to establishing unity in God's spiritual family. Paul writes, "You must make allowance for each other's faults and forgive the person who offends you. Remember, the Lord forgave you, so you must forgive others" (Colossians 3:13). Because everyone in God's spiritual family is still very human, disagreements and wrongdoing will arise. When they do, we must remember how much God has forgiven us, and, in appreciation, bestow the same forgiveness on others so healing can take place.

By demonstrating humility, submission, and forgiveness, you follow Christ's example. And you will be better able to fulfill God's plan.

God Enlisted You to Build Up Others in Christ

The Bible exhorts, "Think of ways to encourage one another to outbursts of love and good deeds" (Hebrews 10:24).

How often do you encourage and challenge fellow Christians to live a life of love and good deeds? God has called you to do just that. His spiritual family will be healthy only if each member lovingly compels the others to become more Christlike and to accomplish God's plan for them.

Henry Ford was once quite discouraged. His newly built combustion engine was criticized and ridiculed because most mechanical experts of his day believed that the "horseless carriage" would be powered by electricity, not gasoline.

One evening, Ford attended a dinner where Thomas Edison was seated several chairs away. As Ford explained his engine to the men near him, Edison overheard. Edison asked Ford to make a sketch of the engine. After studying the drawing, Edison banged his fist on the table. "Young man," he said, "that's the thing! You have it!"

Ford later stated, "The thump of that fist upon the table was worth worlds to me."[4]

Colossians 3:16 declares, "Let the word of Christ dwell in you richly as you teach and admonish one another with all wisdom, and as you sing psalms, hymns and spiritual songs with gratitude in your hearts to God" (NIV). As we feed on the Word of God, we are to exhort each other with God's truth and wisdom. What should our motivation be? Gratitude for all the wonderful blessings God has given us.

As we travel together on the amazing adventure of the Christian life, we are always to consider the needs of our fellow believers, not just our own. The body of Christ has an amazing purpose, and we cannot fulfill God's calling by ourselves. We must work together and stimulate each other to Christlike behavior as we live for Him.

To do this, we must honestly examine ourselves. Ask yourself: Do my words and deeds encourage the people in my local church? Do I spur others to love and good deeds, or do I criticize and tear others down?

God Redeemed You to Love Others

The Bible proclaims, "You can have sincere love for each other as brothers and sisters because you were cleansed from your sins when you accepted the truth of the Good News. So see to it that you really do love each other intensely with all your hearts" (1 Peter 1:22).

God wants the members of His family to love each other. Jesus told His disciples that love would be a hallmark of His church. "I am giving you a new commandment: Love each other. Just as I have loved you, you should love each other. Your love for one another will prove to the world that you are My disciples" (John 13:34,35).

Calvin Hunt was an alcoholic and a drug addict. He worked during the day and got high at night and on weekends. Seeing his wife and children was a painful reminder of how he had failed them and how desperate his life had become.

But his wife prayed for him, as did the members of her church. One night while she and the children were at a prayer meeting, Calvin heard what sounded like people weeping as he lay down to sleep. He checked the closets and under the bed, but no one was there.

Unnerved, he hurried to the church to find his wife. As he entered the sanctuary, the same sound of weeping greeted him. There in intense prayer were Calvin's wife and members of her church. Many of these people had never met him, yet they had been weeping and praying over him for an hour. Their love helped bring Calvin to a new and abundant life in Christ.[5]

When members of the body of Christ love each other, they reflect Christ to the world.

In 1889, a tower was built for an international exposition. The residents of the city called the structure "monstrous" and demanded it be torn down as soon as the exposition was over. Yet from the start, the architect believed in his creation and boldly defended it against those who wanted to destroy it. He believed the tower was destined for greatness.

Today this tower is considered one of the architectural wonders of the modern world, and it is the primary landmark of Paris, France. The architect was Alexandre Gustave Eiffel, and the tower, of course, is the Eiffel Tower.[6]

Jesus has designed a structure that He greatly loves and champions. In the past, He entrusted this unique entity to an unlikely group of disciples. Today He has committed it to our care. Outsiders might view this creation as "monstrous" and believe that we are incapable, but Jesus knows that His structure is destined for greatness.

What is this amazing structure? The Church.

The body of Christ began with the early disciples and stretches into eternity. It cannot be destroyed. Jesus promises His followers, "Upon this rock I will build my church, and all the powers of hell will not conquer it" (Matthew 16:18).

What a privilege to be members of the body of our Lord! How we should cherish our place in His spiritual family.

The next time you attend your local church, see it through the eyes of your loving Father. Commit yourself to use the gifts God has given you to build up your brothers and sisters and promote unity. And above all, determine to love the wonderful community of believers God has chosen.

four

EXPERIENCING SUPERNATURAL POWER

Now glory be to God! By His mighty power at work within us, He is able to accomplish infinitely more than we would ever dare to ask or hope.

EPHESIANS 3:20

"THE 100 MOST Powerful People." This headline dominates the cover of a popular entertainment magazine. Inside, the editors rank film and television moguls and celebrities based on their financial resources and their ability to mastermind megaprojects and close multimillion-dollar deals.

In reading through the list of notables, perhaps you feel a twinge of jealousy. How you wish you were powerful! If you only had more power, you could change your circumstances, influence other people, or feel in control of your life.

But are you so powerless? Is worldly power really what you need?

On a radiant New Year's morning in Pasadena, California, a beautiful float in the Tournament of Roses parade suddenly sputtered and stopped. It was out of gas. The parade came to a standstill until someone brought a few gallons of gasoline.

The irony of the situation was that the float represented the Standard Oil Company. This large corporation owned vast reserves of gas and oil, yet its float came to a grinding halt because it had run out of fuel.[1]

How similar this is to us when we fail to draw upon the vast reserves of our mighty Savior's power, which are so readily available to us through our new identity in Christ.

It Makes All the Difference

In the mid-1800s, an ordinary boy grew up in a small town in Massachusetts. His widowed mother struggled to provide for her nine children. At one point, the family was so poor that the children walked to church barefoot, carrying their shoes and stockings so they would not wear out. At the age of 17, this boy made a commitment to Christ in the back room of the shoe store where he worked. His life was changed. He began inviting everyone he could to his church. When he attempted to preach, one of the deacons assured him that he could serve God best by keeping silent. Another member praised the young man for his zeal, but recommended that he realize his limitations and not attempt to speak in public.

This average young man was named Dwight L. Moody. He went on to preach to millions and to be used by God to draw thousands upon thousands into Christ's kingdom.

"The world has yet to see what God will do with . . . the man who is fully consecrated to Him."

What made the difference in the life of this ordinary man? At the beginning of Moody's ministry, he accepted the challenge of a Mr. Henry Varley: "The world has yet to see what God will do with and for and through and in and by the man who is fully consecrated to Him." Moody thought, "He said 'a man.' He did not say a great man, nor a learned man, nor a smart man, but simply 'a man.' I am a man and it lies within the man himself whether he will or will not make that entire and full consecration."[2]

That day Moody gave all of himself to his Savior and Lord. He invited Christ to live in and through him—and that made all the difference.

Power for Victory

Our victory in Christ, like the victory D. L. Moody experienced, is possible only by living in Christ's power. His power is radically different from and superior to the power of the world. King David declared, "In Your hands are strength and power to exalt and give strength to all" (1 Chronicles 29:12, NIV). Jeremiah exclaimed, "O Sovereign Lord! You have made the heavens and earth by Your great power. Nothing is too hard for You!" (Jeremiah 32:17).

The natural vehicles of power in this world are wealth, authority, popularity, might, and influence. But God's power is supernatural. His power is not limited by human abilities, resources, or intelligence. He is not bound by time or any physical barriers. His power can be awesome, as displayed in the parting of the Red Sea, or serene, as demonstrated by the still, small voice of God.

Often, God may sovereignly use the world's sources of power for His purposes, as He did when He placed Esther in a place of authority to save the Jewish people. But God is not limited by our lack of wealth, influence, position, or prestige. In fact, Christ's power is made perfect in our weakness. Paul exclaims, "I am glad to boast about my weaknesses, so that the power of Christ may work through me" (2 Corinthians 12:9).

God's greatest "power play" was the ultimate act of love, servanthood, and self-sacrifice: Christ's death on the cross and His glorious resurrection. This sacrificial act of supernatural power defeated death and Satan, making it possible for us to have eternal fellowship with our all-powerful God.

If you understand who you are in Christ, you can access His power to reach your spiritual potential. Through Him, you can reach heights you could never attain on your own.

Resources for Spiritual Power

Consider what happens when you board a plane. You say, "I am flying to my destination." But you are not doing the flying; the plane is. You are able to fly only because you are in the plane. If you stepped outside the door, you would plummet to the ground.

In the same way, we have no power in and of ourselves to live the Christian life. It requires supernatural power—the life of Christ living in and through us. If we try to "step outside the plane" and live the Christian life in our own strength, we will fall.

This supernatural life is given to us the moment we are born spiritually. The Bible assures us, "His divine power has given us everything we need for life and godliness through our knowledge of Him who called us by His own glory and goodness" (2 Peter 1:3, NIV).

All believers have three resources for spiritual power: the Holy Spirit, Scripture, and prayer.

You are empowered by the *Holy Spirit* who indwells you. He is the source of all spiritual power. He gives us power to live a supernatural life and be fruitful for God. Note Paul's divinely inspired prayer for the Ephesians: "I pray that from His glorious, unlimited resources He will give you mighty inner strength through His Holy Spirit" (Ephesians 3:16).

In 1947, I was part of a seminary deputation team that spoke in a Los Angeles church. People came up afterward and complemented us. They said, "Oh, you are wonderful. You will make fine ministers." But no one, as far as I know, was challenged to do anything for the Lord.

Later that year, while I was at Forest Home Conference Center in the San Bernardino Mountains, the Holy Spirit gave me insights that transformed my life in a supernatural way. For the first time I really understood what it meant to be filled with the Holy Spirit. I went back to that same church to speak, and when I gave the invitation, practically the whole church came forward weeping. I was speaking with the supernatural power of the Holy Spirit, which made all the difference!

We are also empowered by *God's Word*. The Holy Spirit empowers and transforms us with God's truth. Scripture says, "The word of God is full of living power. It is sharper than the sharpest knife, cutting deep into our innermost thoughts and desires. It exposes us for what we really are" (Hebrews 4:12).

Martin Luther's life was transformed by the power of God's Word. As a student and later as a monk, he suffered from fits of severe depression. We do not know what physiological or psychological factors may have been involved, but we do know that he was desperately seeking assurance of his salvation.

Although Luther poured himself into his studies, received a doctorate in theology, and became a professor of Scripture, his agony continued. Then one night, the Spirit opened his eyes to the marvelous truth of Romans 1:17: "the just shall live by faith" (KJV). Hope and peace filled his heart.

The Bible assured Luther that salvation was not determined by his good works, but only by faith in Christ—and the Reformation was born. God's truth powerfully transformed Luther's life and the world.

We are also empowered through *prayer*. Prayer releases God's power in our lives. Scripture commands, "Devote yourselves to prayer with an alert mind and a thankful heart" (Colossians 4:2).

Shortly after its founding, Dallas Seminary faced a severe financial crisis. One morning, its founders met to pray knowing that at noon that day all the creditors would foreclose. Harry Ironside, who was in that meeting, prayed, "Lord, we know that the cattle on a thousand hills are thine. Please sell some of them and send us the money."

As they prayed in the seminary president's office, a tall Texan showed up in the business office with a check in his hand. He explained that he had sold some cattle and had planned to use the money for a business deal, but the deal did not work out. He felt God wanted the money given to the seminary.

A secretary brought the check to the prayer meeting. The amount was exactly what the seminary owed. The president, Lewis Sperry Chafer, recognized the name on the check. Turning to Dr. Ironside, he said, "Harry, God sold the cattle."[3]

Prayer involves praising and thanking God, listening to Him, and seeking His will to accomplish His purposes. Obviously, it was God's purpose for Dallas Seminary to continue. Since that day, God has used this seminary to train tens of thousands of pastors, missionaries, teachers, and other ministers.

God wants us to use His power for His purposes today. Let's look at five reasons why God gives us power. With the acrostic POWER, you can remember that God gives you power to...

P *Proclaim* the gospel boldly

O *Overcome* evil forces in the world and the spiritual realm

W *Withstand* personal temptation

E *Embrace* God's perfect will for your life

R *Reflect* God's character

Power to Proclaim the Gospel Boldly

Jesus explained to His followers, "When the Holy Spirit has come upon you, you will receive power and will tell people about Me everywhere—in Jerusalem, throughout Judea, in Samaria, and to the ends of the earth" (Acts 1:8).

God has empowered us to be His witnesses, even in the most difficult circumstances.

Paul and Silas traveled to Philippi to share the good news of Jesus' death and resurrection. But rather than rejoicing at the wonderful news of a right relationship with the only true God, the Philippian magistrates had Paul and Silas severely beaten and thrown in prison.

How did Paul and Silas respond? As they lay in their cell, their feet in stocks and their backs bloody, they did not hate their enemies or feel despair. Instead, they prayed, sang hymns, and proclaimed Christ to those around them. As a result, the jailer and his family were saved, and a great work began in Philippi.

This same Holy Spirit motivates and empowers believers today. On any given day, it is estimated that as many as 2,000 teams are showing the *JESUS* film in villages, cities, and universities around the world. These teams consist of courageous, godly men and women who in certain parts of the world risk their lives to share the wonderful message of Jesus Christ. Because these brave believers love God so much, they refuse to remain silent as long as there are people who have not heard the gospel. Many have been stoned; others have been poisoned; some even killed. These dedicated Christians have helped take the gospel through the *JESUS* film to more than 3.5 billion people.

Words apart from the power of God are simply words. But as we draw upon His power, the words of the gospel will penetrate the minds and hearts of those around us.

Power to Overcome Evil Forces in the World and the Spiritual Realm

The Bible explains, "Every child of God defeats this evil world by trusting Christ to give the victory. And the ones who win this battle against the world are the ones who believe that Jesus is the Son of God" (1 John 5:4,5).

God's power working in and through us surpasses all worldly and evil forces.

The Old Testament prophet Elijah relied on God's power to prevail against strongholds of deception. King Ahab had turned many of the people away from God to worship Baal.

But Elijah stood up to the king and hundreds of false prophets. He proposed a power demonstration. Two bulls would be placed on altars as

sacrifices. Whoever consumed a bull by fire—
Baal or the God of Israel—was God indeed.

The prophets of Baal cried out to their god,
cut themselves, and danced around their altar,
but nothing happened. Then Elijah ordered that
the bull on the altar of the LORD be soaked with
water. As he prayed, God sent down fire from
heaven and consumed the bull, as well as the sur-
rounding wood, stones, and soil. When the Israel-
ites saw this, they all fell pros-
trate and cried, "The LORD is
God! The LORD is God!" (1
Kings 18:39). As a result, the
prophets of Baal were put to
death, for their deception had
been revealed.

Satan's primary weapon is
deception. But the power of
God's truth can defang the lies
of the adversary. Scripture says, "We are human,
but we don't wage war with human plans and
methods. We use God's mighty weapons, not mere
worldly weapons, to knock down the Devil's
strongholds. With these weapons we break down
every proud argument that keeps people from
knowing God. With these weapons we conquer

*Simply serving
God was not
enough. I longed to
possess a heart
overflowing with
love and praise
for my Lord.*

their rebellious ideas, and we teach them to obey Christ" (2 Corinthians 10:3–5).

Power to Withstand Personal Temptation

The Bible assures us, "The temptations that come into your life are no different from what others experience. And God is faithful. He will keep the temptation from becoming so strong that you can't stand up against it. When you are tempted, He will show you a way out so that you will not give in to it" (1 Corinthians 10:13).

God's power is strong enough to help us resist any temptation.

When Jesus was tempted by Satan in the wilderness, He relied on the power of God's Word. He resisted Satan's propaganda by quoting Scripture. Satan offered Jesus the kingdoms of the world, tempted Him to use His power to satisfy His desires, and suggested that Jesus test God to prove His own deity. But Jesus withstood the temptation and chose to gain power God's way— by dying on the cross.

The power of God's Word is also available to you. The Spirit of the living Christ—the One who successfully resisted Satan in the wilderness— lives in you.

You may be tempted by pornography, addictions, or other things that lead you astray from wholeheartedly loving and serving your wonderful Savior. Scripture warns, "Do not be deceived: God cannot be mocked. A man reaps what he sows. The one who sows to please his sinful nature, from that nature will reap destruction; the one who sows to please the Spirit, from the Spirit will reap eternal life" (Galatians 6:7,8, NIV). When you disobey God, you will reap consequences—broken hearts, missed opportunities, and shattered lives. But Christ in you is stronger than any temptation. When facing temptation, remember the many promises of Scripture and rely on the Holy Spirit to empower you. Then stand firm!

Power to Embrace God's Perfect Will for Your Life

Through God's power, we can accomplish much more than the goals and plans possible by human means. Scripture promises, "Now glory be to God! By His mighty power at work within us, He is able to accomplish infinitely more than we would ever dare to ask or hope" (Ephesians 3:20).

Our mighty God empowers us to complete our life quest. Jesus' disciples learned this firsthand when He asked them to feed more than five thousand men, women, and children with five loaves and two fish.

Imagine feeding thousands of people with this little bit of food! The disciples thought it impossible, but Jesus took their meager resources, blessed them, and gave them back to the disciples.

As the disciples obeyed the Lord and distributed the food, it multiplied. Everyone was fed. And there were twelve baskets of food left over!

If we place ourselves and all we have into God's hands, He will bless and multiply our efforts and resources to accomplish His purposes. He will empower us to accomplish what He desires in the fulfillment of His will—including living a godly life.

Power to Reflect God's Character

Paul prayed for the Colossians, "We also pray that you will be strengthened with His glorious power so that you will have all the patience and endurance you need" (Colossians 1:11).

God empowers us to become more like His holy Son.

Peter was strengthened with God's mighty power. He went from denying Christ three times to being a mighty leader of the early Church. Through the power of the Holy Spirit, he was used by God to bring 3,000 people to Christ at Pentecost, and he was the first to spread the gospel to the Gentiles. When Peter was martyred for his faith, he refused to die the same way as his glorious Savior, so the soldiers crucified him upside down. Although Peter began his journey with Jesus as an impulsive, rugged fisherman, he died a mirror of the One he so loved.

Peter is an example of how the power of God can be manifested in an ordinary person's life. Though he lacked worldly wealth and influence, he allowed himself to be a channel for God's power. Because of his yieldedness, he had a tremendous spiritual impact that continues today.

You and I may feel very ordinary at times, but Christ in us makes all the difference. Scripture promises, "Those who wait on the LORD will find new strength. They will fly high on wings like eagles. They will run and not grow weary. They will walk and not faint" (Isaiah 40:31).

While on this earth, you may feel powerless, but you must always remember the source of all power is the Master of the universe. His power is available to all who know and seek Him.

five

ACHIEVING TRIUMPH
OVER ADVERSITY

For when your faith is tested, your endur-
ance has a chance to grow.
JAMES 1:3

WITHOUT WARNING, something can happen to
you that changes your life forever: A loved one is
disabled by an accident or illness. A child dies. A
marriage crumbles. A fire, flood, or earthquake
destroys your home.

How do you react? Do you fall apart? Do you
become bitter? Do you question God?

About twenty years ago, a young woman entered into a lifetime of severe suffering. Joni Eareckson Tada dove into a lake and broke her neck.
When she resurfaced, she had to be pulled from
the water. Since then Joni has had no feeling or
movement in her arms or legs. The suffering she
faced and continues to experience is undoubtedly more than most of us will ever understand.

In her sorrow, Joni asked a question that I am

sure all of us have pondered when going through great difficulty or tragedy: "What possible good can come out of what I am now going through?" She also asked, "Why me?"

"The suffering and pain," Joni says, "have helped me mature emotionally, mentally, and spiritually. Pain and suffering have purpose. I believe God was working in my life to create grace and wisdom out of the chaos of pain and depression."[1]

More Than Conquerors

Thousands of years earlier, a Hebrew young man named Daniel had his life changed forever by tragedy. His people were conquered by King Nebuchadnezzar of Babylon. Daniel was taken from his homeland of Judah to a foreign country to be trained for service to this pagan ruler.

Although his life was turned upside down, Daniel knew one thing had not changed. God is the same yesterday, today, and forever. Daniel put his faith in the Lord, and overcame his conqueror. He won the king's favor and respect. Nebuchadnezzar came to rely on Daniel's wisdom and admire his faith. Some maintain this pagan ruler eventually came to faith in God.

Nebuchadnezzar was a conqueror, but Daniel

was more than a conqueror. Scripture triumphantly proclaims that this same victory belongs to all who are in Christ. God assures us, "Who shall separate us from the love of Christ? Shall trouble or hardship or persecution or famine or nakedness or danger or sword?...No, in all these things we are more than conquerors through Him who loved us" (Romans 8:35,37, NIV).

Let us look at four compelling biblical reasons that we are more than conquerors:

- Jesus Christ is more than a conqueror.

- We are in Christ.

- Nothing can separate us from Christ's love.

- God makes sure we cannot lose.

First, *we are more than conquerors because Jesus is more than a conqueror.* Our Savior suffered overwhelming adversity and through it transformed the world. Listen to this prophetic description of the Messiah from the Old Testament book of Isaiah:

> *He was despised and rejected—a man of sorrows, acquainted with bitterest grief. We turned our backs on Him and looked the other way when*

He went by. He was despised, and we did not care. Yet it was our weaknesses He carried; it was our sorrows that weighed Him down. And we thought His troubles were a punishment from God for His own sins! But He was wounded and crushed for our sins. He was beaten that we might have peace. He was whipped, and we were healed (Isaiah 53:3–5).

Jesus endured temptation without sinning so He could be the perfect sacrifice for our sins (Hebrews 4:15). He endured rejection and persecution to make us acceptable to God. He defeated death through His resurrection so we could live with Him forever. He loved us while we were still His enemies so we could become His friends.

Secondly, *we are more than conquerors because we are in Christ.* Jesus conquered sin and death, and we are now in Him. We share in His marvelous victory! Paul writes, "How we thank God, who gives us victory over sin and death through Jesus Christ our Lord!" (1 Corinthians 15:57). Scripture also promises, "Everyone born of God overcomes the world. This is the victory that has overcome the world, even our faith" (1 John 5:4, NIV). Jesus Christ's power working in us ensures victory over anything this life may bring us.

Third, *we are more than conquerors because nothing can separate us from Christ's love.* Just listen to this magnificent promise from Romans 8:38,39:

> *I am convinced that nothing can ever separate us from His love. Death can't, and life can't. The angels can't, and the demons can't. Our fears for today, our worries about tomorrow, and even the powers of hell can't keep God's love away. Whether we are high above the sky or in the deepest ocean, nothing in all creation will ever be able to separate us from the love of God that is revealed in Christ Jesus our Lord.*

No spiritual force or being can ever separate us from His amazing love. No tragedy or difficult circumstance can ever remove us from the presence of Christ's love. It does not matter where we go on earth or even in space, we can never go beyond the boundary of His all-encompassing love.

Finally, *we are more than conquerors because God makes sure we cannot lose.* God gives us this magnificent assurance in Romans 8:28: "We know that God causes everything to work together for the good of those who love God and are called according to His purpose for them."

God does not promise that only good things

will happen to His children. But He does promise that whatever happens He will use for our eternal benefit. We may not always understand the reason for difficulties in our life, but God can and will use bad things to make us better (James 1:2–4).

Pearls are formed when a tiny foreign particle, such as a grain of sand, finds its way into an oyster shell, causing irritation. This aggravation triggers secretions that form a magnificent gem.

The adversity we face in this world is like a grain of sand rubbing us the wrong way. It gets our attention. And if we are walking with Christ, it makes us rethink our priorities and triggers character growth. Our problems—although sometimes overwhelming in this life—are insignificant compared to the marvelous future glory that awaits us in our Lord and Savior, Jesus Christ.

Let us now look at seven benefits God brings out of adversity. With the acrostic TRIUMPH, you can remember that God uses adversity to produce...

T *Training* in obedience

R *Refinement* of your character

I *Intimacy* with your compassionate God and Savior

U *Understanding* of the hurts of others

M *Maturity* for ministering to others

P *Perseverance* in difficult times

H *Hope* for the future

Adversity Produces Training in Obedience

Scripture declares, "Even though Jesus was God's Son, He learned obedience from the things He suffered" (Hebrews 5:8). We often learn the most in the midst of adversity.

A dear friend of mine whom I had the privilege of introducing to our Savior became one of the most prominent business leaders in his state. In time, this successful, influential man became ill with cancer. As his body was ravaged with disease, he and his wife drew closer and closer to Christ. They read the Scriptures and sang hymns of praise throughout the day. On several occasions he said to me, "I'm so glad I have cancer because it was only when I discovered I was seriously ill that my relationship with Christ really became intimate. I had known about Christ and had received Him. I went through the ritual of being a Christian, but somehow it was not until I became ill and faced my eternal destiny that I looked up and saw the loving, forgiving grace of God."

I had the privilege of taking part in my friend's memorial service. It was a time of celebration because this great man, who had known the best the world could offer, came to know the best God has to offer—through adversity.

Adversity brings us to the end of ourselves and drives us to God. It teaches us about ourselves and our Lord. As the Puritan Thomas Watson wrote, "A sick-bed often teaches more than a sermon."[2]

Adversity Produces Refinement of Your Character

In a marvelous Scripture verse, Psalm 119:71, we read, "The suffering You sent was good for me, for it taught me to pay attention to Your principles."

The triumph of adversity is often expressed in a renewed walk with God and a refinement of our character.

The Bible compares God's work of maturing us to the process of refining precious metal. Ore is subjected to tremendous heat and liquefied so impurities can be removed. In a similar way, the heat of adversity softens us so that God can do

His work of refinement and sanctification. Adversity is the touchstone of character. Hardship reveals our strengths and weaknesses. If we have been out of fellowship with God, He may use hard times to restore us. If we are weak, He may use difficulties to strengthen us.

Consider the following true story from *Leadership* magazine:

> When he was seven years old, his family was forced out of their home on a legal technicality, and he had to work to help support them. At age nine, his mother died. At 22, he lost his job as a store clerk. He wanted to go to law school, but his education was not good enough. At 23, he went into debt to become a partner in a small store. At 26, his business partner died, leaving him a huge debt that took years to repay.
>
> At 28, after courting a girl for four years, he asked her to marry him. She said no. At 37, on his third try, he was elected to Congress, but two years later, he failed to be re-elected. At 41, his four-year-old son died. At 45, he ran for the Senate and lost. At 47, he failed as the vice-presidential candidate. At 49, he ran for the Senate again, and lost.[3]

Who was this man? He was a person whom many hail as the greatest leader America has ever had—Abraham Lincoln. Consider all the hardships Lincoln faced before becoming president of the United States at the age of 51. These difficulties were not merely footnotes on the way to his election to presidential office. No, they are what built his character. God allowed trials to prepare him to lead America during a time of great national adversity.

Adversity Produces Intimacy with Your Compassionate God and Savior

The biblical character of Job has become synonymous with suffering. After enduring tremendous adversity, Job told God, "I had heard about You before, but now I have seen You with my own eyes" (Job 42:5).

Through adversity, God can deepen our relationship with Him.

In the 1940s, I owned a specialty-foods firm in Los Angeles. One of my partners in the business was a member of my church, and while I was studying at Princeton, I hired his son to oversee the company's daily operations. When I returned from my studies, I found the business greatly changed and discovered that several members of my partner's family were drawing upon our investment! The family became defensive and accused me of being dishonest and not fulfilling my financial commitments to them.

Finally, the situation came to the attention of the pastor of our church. I was cleared of all accusations, but was still haunted by the thought that members in my church may have been influenced by this family's gossip and that they now saw me as phony or dishonest. I moved out of my apartment and lived in the company's plant to save money so I could buy out this partner. There I spent many evenings grieving about the situation.

Several years later, I was nominated to be a deacon at my church. As soon as my name was mentioned, my former business partner stood up and accused me of being dishonest. Another family member said that I was "not worthy of such a responsible trust."

You can imagine the pain I felt as a congregation of more than a thousand people heard those accusations. My pastor quickly ushered the nominating committee into another room to discuss the situation. I hurried to the room and begged them to withdraw my name. But my pastor assured the committee that he knew about the situation and that the accusations against me were not true. He insisted my name remain on the list of deacons.

At that moment, a woman entered the room and announced, "I don't know what the issues are, but I know this: I wouldn't be a Christian today if it weren't for Bill Bright."

The committee returned to the sanctuary, and when it was announced that my nomination would remain on the list, the congregation burst into applause. Those around me rose to their feet, and the many days and nights of doubt and discouragement faded away.

God was humbling me, polishing me, and preparing me for a vision He was soon to give me, which became Campus Crusade for Christ. Had I not gone through that experience, I doubt seriously if God could have used me for any holy purpose.

The more adversity we go through with God, the more we learn how faithful He is to help us in our time of need.

Adversity Produces Understanding of the Hurts of Others

Scripture says of Jesus, "This High Priest of ours understands our weaknesses, for He faced all of the same temptations we do, yet He did not sin" (Hebrews 4:15).

Experiencing adversity allows us to understand and empathize with those who are hurting.

A store owner placed a sign in his window announcing "Puppies for Sale." Soon a small boy came with $2.37 to buy a puppy. The store owner chuckled at the boy's enthusiasm and agreed to let the boy take a look at the litter. When the mother and her pups bounded out of the kennel, one of the puppies lagged behind. The man explained that the puppy had a malformed hip socket and would always limp.

The boy excitedly announced that he wanted to buy the limping puppy. He gave the owner the $2.37 and told him he would pay on the balance every month until he had paid for the dog.

The man tried to discourage the child, warning that the puppy would never run, jump, and play with him like other puppies. To that, the boy pulled up his pant leg and revealed a left leg supported by a metal brace. He said, "I know how he feels. He'll need someone who understands."[4]

Adversity humbles us and softens our hearts so we are more compassionate and understanding of others.

Adversity Produces Maturity for Ministering to Others

The Word of God gives this challenge: "So take a new grip with your tired hands and stand firm on your shaky legs. Mark out a straight path for your feet. Then those who follow you, though they are weak and lame, will not stumble and fall but will become strong" (Hebrews 12:12,13).

Adversity prods us to grow and prepares us to minister to others.

When a mother eagle builds her nest, she begins with unlikely materials: rocks, thorns, and bits of broken branches. Before laying her eggs, she blankets the nest with feathers and fur from animals she has killed. This soft, downy nest makes a perfect home for her eggs. Her growing young are so comfortable that when they are old enough to fly, they are reluctant to leave. That is when the mother eagle begins to "stir up the nest." She uses her talons to rip up the lining of feathers and fur, revealing the broken branches and sharp rocks underneath. The nest becomes uncomfortable for her young, prompting them to fly away to pursue the life of mature eagles.[5]

Sometimes God "stirs up the nest" to encourage us to step out of our comfort zone and to mature us in areas we have not encountered before. Hardships make us grow in our understanding of ourselves, others, and our wonderful God. When we emerge victorious on the other side of our "valley of adversity," we are better able to live as we should and to encourage others in the often bumpy journey of life.

Adversity Produces Perseverance in Difficult Times

Scripture tells us, "When your faith is tested, your endurance has a chance to grow" (James 1:3).

God often uses adversity to strengthen our resolve and solidify our commitment to Him.

One of the greatest examples of perseverance took place in England during World War II. At the war's beginning, Neville Chamberlain was the prime minister. As the Nazis swarmed Austria, Poland, Czechoslovakia, and even threatened the shores of Great Britain, Chamberlain tried to appease them.

But when Winston Churchill took the helm, he inaugurated his term as prime minister with these words:

> *I have nothing to offer but blood, toil, tears, and sweat. We have before us an ordeal of the*

*most grievous kind. We have before us many,
many months of struggle and suffering. You ask,
what is our policy? I say it is to wage war by
land, sea and air. War with all our might and
with all the strength God has given us, and to
wage war against a monstrous tyranny never
surpassed in the dark and lamentable catalogue
of human crime. That is our policy. You ask,
what is our aim? I can answer in one word. It is
victory. Victory at all costs—victory in spite of
all terrors—victory, however long and hard the
road may be, for without victory there is no sur-
vival.*[6]

Churchill's words ring of perseverance. As si-
rens sounded and bombs pounded Great Britain,
he told his people to "never give up."

Are you in the midst of a divorce? Do you have
cancer or another deadly disease? Are you worried about your financial situation? No matter how
"long and hard the road may be," God will give
you the strength necessary to persevere.

Adversity Produces Hope for the Future

The Bible promises, "We also rejoice in our suf-
ferings, because we know that suffering produces
perseverance; perseverance, character; and char-

acter, hope. And hope does not disappoint us, because God has poured out His love into our hearts by the Holy Spirit, whom He has given us" (Romans 5:3,4, NIV).

The marvelous truth of Scripture is that, for Christians, suffering leads to hope.

Author Halford E. Luccock penned these words: "Where there is no faith in the future, there is no power in the present."[7] No matter what our circumstances may be, as Christians we have every reason to have faith in the future because God has promised His beloved children a glorious inheritance and a future of intimate fellowship with Him. Because we can look forward to the future without fear, we can live victoriously today. We know who holds our future, and He is faithful.

six

POSSESSING INFINITE JOY

> *I have told you this so that you will be*
> *filled with My joy. Yes, your joy will over-*
> *flow!*
>
> JOHN 15:11

WHEN YOU HEAR the word "joy," what comes to mind? A giggling child cuddling with her father? A young couple, their eyes filled with love, standing at the marriage altar? A beaming athlete holding up a glistening trophy? An elated woman winning the lottery?

Many people believe that joy can be acquired through the treasures and perks of this world—a thrilling adventure, a satisfying achievement, or some pleasing acquisition. However, they will be sorely disappointed by their false hopes.

Jay Gould, one of America's leading financiers, failed to find joy in his money. With his own death approaching, he said, "I suppose I am the most miserable man on earth."

The famous poet Lord Byron failed to find joy in a life of pleasure. He wrote, "The worm, the canker, and grief are mine alone."

French philosopher and author Voltaire failed to find joy in intellectual pursuits. He wrote: "I wish I had never been born."

Lord Beaconsfield, 19th century British politician and prime minister, failed to find joy in his fame and position. He wrote, "Youth is a mistake; manhood a struggle; old age a regret."

Alexander the Great failed to find joy in military glory. After he had subdued all his enemies, he wept and said, "There are no more worlds to conquer."[1]

Many of the most wealthy, famous, intelligent, and influential people have failed to experience true joy. Undoubtedly, they have enjoyed periods of happiness, but happiness depends upon circumstances, and once hardships arise, happiness gives way to worry and discontent. However, true joy abides even when life is difficult and unsure.

What Is Joy?

Paul wrote the Book of Philippians—an epistle filled with the message of joy and hope—from a prison cell. How could he be joyful even when he was in confinement? It is because joy is not found in circumstances. Deep, abiding joy is found only in an intimate relationship with the source of all joy—Jesus Christ.

The *Life Application Bible Commentary* defines joy this way: "Joy is the gladdening of the heart that comes from knowing Christ as Lord, the feeling of relief because we are released from sin; it is the inner peace and tranquility we have because we know the final outcome of our lives; and it is the assurance that God is in us and in every circumstance."[2]

Joy flows out of our relationship with Christ.

At the birth of Christ, an angel triumphantly proclaimed: "I bring you good news of great joy for everyone! The Savior—yes, the Messiah, the Lord—has been born tonight in Bethlehem, the city of David!" (Luke 2:10,11).

God became man and died to pay the penalty for our sins. What a reason for rejoicing! Because of Christ's great sacrifice, we have been made right with our all-powerful Creator. We have a new identity. We are God's dearly loved children, heirs of His incredible blessings, saints with a new nature, members of the body of Christ, and citizens of Christ's kingdom. Because of Jesus Christ, we can live in friendship with our magnificent God and be filled with His Holy Spirit. When we grasp the magnitude of this marvelous truth, we, too, will rejoice with the shepherds!

Once we understand our new identity and invite Christ to live His life in and through us, joy will abound. For joy is a fruit produced by Christ's Spirit working in us (Galatians 5:22). An apple tree—if it is healthy and receives sufficient sunshine, water, and nutrients—will bear apples. It was created and designed for that purpose. In the same way, if we, as children of God, depend on the Holy Spirit to feed and nourish us, we will experience the fruit of joy in our lives.

Joy is the natural result of living a Christlike life. As we think with the mind of Christ, we will dwell on noble, uplifting thoughts that nurture joy. As we speak with the words of Christ, we will cultivate joy in our heart and the hearts of others. As we behave with the character of Christ, we will reap joy as a benefit of leading a godly life.

British scholar and writer C. S. Lewis expresses it well: "Our Lord finds our desires not too strong, but too weak. We are half-hearted creatures, fooling about with drink and sex and ambition, when infinite joy is offered to us, like an ignorant child who wants to go on making mud pies in the slum because he cannot imagine what is meant by the offer of a holiday at the sea. We are far too easily pleased."[3]

Because of who Jesus Christ is and who you are in Him, you have a threefold source of joy. The acrostic JOY can help you remember to experience joy in...

J *Jesus*
O *Others*
Y *Yourself*

Joy in Jesus

The Bible tells us, "Since we were restored to friendship with God by the death of His Son while we were still His enemies, we will certainly be delivered from eternal punishment by His life. So now we can rejoice in our wonderful new relationship with God—all because of what our Lord Jesus Christ has done for us in making us friends of God" (Romans 5:10,11).

We can experience joy in Jesus because He is our Savior, not our slayer.

We were enemies of God worthy only of death and eternal punishment. But instead of condemning us, Christ gave Himself to be crucified for our sins. Now instead of everlasting damnation, we enjoy eternal blessings in Christ. Because of Jesus, we can know constant joy in our salvation and have fellowship with God.

The well-known conductor Reichel was leading his choir and orchestra through a rehearsal of Handel's glorious masterpiece, *The Messiah*. The soprano soloist sang the inspiring aria, "I Know That My Redeemer Liveth," with flawless technique, effortless breathing, and clear diction. When she finished, everyone turned to Reichel expecting a pleased response. Instead, he motioned for silence and walked over to the soloist. Sorrowfully, he said, "My daughter, you do not really know that your Redeemer lives, do you?"

Embarrassed, she replied, "Why, yes, I think I do."

"Then sing it!" he cried. "Tell it to me so that I'll know you have experienced the joy and power of it."

He raised his baton for the orchestra to begin, and the soloist sang the truth with a passion that revealed her personal knowledge of the risen Lord. Many who were listening wept, and Reichel, his eyes moist with tears, said to her, "You do know, for this time you have told me."[4]

God has given us a wonderful gift in His Son,

Jesus. How we should thank, praise, and worship Him for Jesus! Only because of His Son's sacrifice in our behalf can we experience God's presence both now and for eternity! King David foretold this great promise: "You will show me the way of life, granting me the joy of Your presence and the pleasures of living with You forever" (Psalm 16:11). Great joy comes from being in our Savior's presence, knowing that we are no longer enemies of God.

Joy in Others

Many passages of Scripture record the great joy Paul took in those to whom he ministered. In 1 Thessalonians, we read, "After all, what gives us hope and joy, and what is our proud reward and crown? It is you! Yes, you will bring us much joy as we stand together before our Lord Jesus when He comes back again. For you are our pride and joy" (2:19,20).

In Christ, we can experience joy in others because they are *opportunities* for ministry, not *obstacles* in our way.

More than two hundred years ago, a young Oxford man mounted the stairs of a monument called the "Market Cross" in the center of Liverpool, England. He leaned against the cross and gazed out at the industrial ghetto before him. The streets teamed with dirty miners and sea-hardened sailors cursing, drinking, and fighting in drunken brawls. After whispering a prayer, the young man opened his mouth and sang:

> O, for a thousand tongues to sing,
> My great Redeemer's praise.
> The glories of my God and King,
> The triumphs of His grace.

The heads of the masses turned toward him because the melody was a popular tune. They listened to the words that fell easily from his lips—words he had authored in honor of the first anniversary of his conversion to Jesus Christ.

As the young man continued singing, the bickering stopped. The brawling was silenced. Never before had the masses heard such a note of joy in anything religious. To them, church was a boring ritual reserved for the pious and the old. To them, religion was for the saved, not for the damned like themselves. To them, God was a distant watchmaker who wound His creation and left it running without caring what happened to the world.

The man was well-known songwriter Charles Wesley. No wonder he captivated their attention. His joyful hymn spoke of a God of love who offered forgiveness and grace for all through His Son, Jesus Christ. Because of Charles Wesley, the teaming masses in Liverpool felt the power of Christ's joy![5]

When we see people through the loving eyes of our Father, we, too, will experience the power of joy. We will see nonbelievers as wonderful opportunities to share Christ's love. Rather than condemning them, we will rejoice in the forgiveness and life-changing possibilities they can experience if they will only invite God to work in their lives.

When we fellowship with our Christian brothers and sisters, we will see them as opportunities for ministry, for only together can we build up the body of Christ and reach out to a despairing world. Rather than becoming jealous or competitive, we will take joy in what Christ is doing in their lives. We will not despair because another believer has more power, spiritual fruit, or money than we do. Instead, we will rejoice that our sovereign and loving Father is working in and through them to further the kingdom of Christ.

Joy in Yourself

Jesus said, "I have loved you even as the Father has loved Me. Remain in My love. When you obey Me, you remain in My love, just as I obey My Father and remain in His love. I have told you this so that you will be filled with My joy. Yes, your joy will overflow!" (John 15:9–11).

We can experience joy because, through the Holy Spirit, we are yearning for God with our new nature, not yoked to sin by our old nature.

Many years ago, I met with the heads of several Christian organizations—InterVarsity, Young Life, Youth for Christ, Navigators, and others. We had a marvelous time of rejoicing in the Lord. Soon it was my time to give a devotion. As I was reading from one of my favorite passages, John 17, which is our Lord's high priestly prayer, I was suddenly gripped with something I had read on numerous occasions, but had never really seen before. Jesus prays to the Father, "I have given them the glory You gave Me, so that they may be one, as We are—I in them and You in Me, all being perfected into one. Then the world will know that You sent Me and will understand that *You love them as much as You love Me*" (John 17:22,23).

I was so ecstatic that I wanted to jump up and

shout. To think that the great Creator God and Father of the universe loves a little old nobody, a sinful person conceived in sin, as much as He loves Jesus! This was more than my finite mind could comprehend. Yet our Savior, who loved us so much that He died for us, says it is so. Oh, how God loves us!

Yes, we still stumble and fall short of the expectations we have for ourselves, but God loves us! He has adopted us and endowed us with immeasurable blessings. Once we understand our amazing identity in Christ, we have ample reason to rejoice in who we are and to praise our wonderful Savior who has made this all possible.

Once we grasp our amazing identity in Christ, we have ample reason to praise our wonderful Savior.

In the third century, a dying man wrote these words to a friend: "It's a bad world, an incredibly bad world. But I have discovered in the midst of it a quiet, holy people who have learned a great secret. They have found a joy which is a thousand times better than any pleasure of our sinful life. They are despised and persecuted, but they care not…They have overcome the world. These people are Christians—and I am one of them."[6]

The Joy-Breakers

How wonderful to experience a joy that need not be limited by favorable circumstances. Yet many of us do not consistently enjoy this blessing. Why is this true? There are several "joy-breakers" that can short-circuit our joy and cause us to wallow in despair and frustration.

One joy-breaker is worry. An old man was once asked what had most robbed him of joy in his life. He answered, "Things that never happened!" How true it is that worry about the future steals our joy today. That is why Jesus said, "Therefore do not worry about tomorrow, for tomorrow will worry about itself. Each day has enough trouble of its own" (Matthew 6:34, NIV).

Another joy-breaker is disobedience to God. It steals our joy by harming the source of all joy— our relationship with God. Joy is a fruit of the Spirit, and we can only bear fruit as we abide in Christ. Jesus said, "A branch cannot produce fruit if it is severed from the vine, and you cannot be fruitful apart from Me" (John 15:4).

Our sin severs us from the vine. Now, we are not removed from God's love, nor is our salvation in doubt; however, until we repent of the sin, the sweet nourishment of the Holy Spirit cannot fill us as He desires. We cannot deliberately disobey God and continue to abide in Christ. Just as a disobedient child cannot be happy knowing he has disappointed his parents, so we cannot be joyful until we have repented and restored our intimacy with our merciful heavenly Father.

A third joy-breaker is guilt. After King David sinned by committing adultery with Bathsheba, he wrote these words, "When I refused to confess my sin, I was weak and miserable, and I groaned all day long. Day and night Your hand of discipline was heavy on me. My strength evaporated like water in the summer heat. Finally, I confessed all my sins to You and stopped trying to hide them. I said to myself, 'I will confess my rebellion to the LORD.' And You forgave me! All my guilt is gone. Therefore, let all the godly confess their rebellion to You while there is time, that they may not drown in the floodwaters of judgment" (Psalm 32:3–6).

A fourth joy-breaker is the failure to seek God wholeheartedly. Seeking God wholeheartedly refers to the quality of our love, desire, and devotion to Him. When we seek God with our whole heart, our desire for closeness with Him becomes increasingly consuming. Our joy grows as our love for our Lord becomes more intimate.

Our relationship with our Creator will only grow as far as our desire permits. Hebrews 11:6 states, "[God] rewards those who sincerely seek Him." There are great rewards in seeking our glorious Creator. The Word of God promises in Psalm 34:10, "Those who trust in the LORD will never lack any good thing." We should seek God wholeheartedly so that we can experience the intimacy with Him that He desires and develop a passion for Him and His purposes. When we strive to love the Lord our God with all of our heart, soul, and mind (Matthew 22:37), we will reap the abundant joy that comes from a deep, contented relationship with almighty God.

Our relationship with our Creator will only grow as far as our desire permits.

When the Jews returned from exile, they wept because of Israel's great sin. Nehemiah encouraged them, "The joy of the LORD is your strength!" (Nehemiah 8:10). We, too, can be comforted by the strength of God's supernatural joy. We can take joy in our amazing Savior whose sacrifice allows us to experience grace, forgiveness, and an eternal life of intimate fellowship with our Creator. We can enjoy others because they are precious souls with whom we can share His joy. And we can rejoice in the work that God has done in our lives because we have a new identity in Christ.

One day we will enter into the heavenlies and stand before Jesus. How wonderful it will be to hear the words, "Well done, my good and faithful servant. You have been faithful in handling this small amount, so now I will give you many more responsibilities. Let's celebrate together!" (Matthew 25:21). What eternal happiness and joy will be ours if we faithfully serve our Lord and Savior!

Praise God for the unspeakable joy of His abundant blessings! May we delight in what we have in Him: an eternal Father and Savior; an eternal inheritance; an eternal holiness; an eternal family; and an eternal kingdom.

What a marvelous identity we have in Christ. In His power we can think, speak, and behave in a way that reaps a life of power, freedom, triumph, peace, and joy. What wonderful blessings! And what a supernatural life we should be living.

Yet, there is one whose deepest desire is to keep us from experiencing the glorious life Christ offers. We will talk about him and how to overcome his evil schemes in our final chapter.

seven

STANDING VICTORIOUSLY IN CHRIST

> *You, dear children, are from God and have overcome them, because the one who is in you is greater than the one who is in the world.*
>
> 1 JOHN 4:4, NIV

THE HOLY SPIRIT empowers us to live extraordinary lives that reflect our new identity in Christ. As we allow Christ to live in and through us, we will experience a life of supernatural power, triumph over adversity, and infinite joy. What an incredible adventure awaits us in Christ! Nothing this world offers compares to our supernatural life in Him.

Our Great Enemy

Yet, there is one who longs to steal the knowledge we have of our glorious new identity in Christ and replace it with doubt, fear, confusion, and insecurity. He desires to kill the righteous thoughts, words, and deeds that come from a Christlike character and replace them with what is hateful, bitter, divisive, hurtful, and degrading. He seeks to destroy the supernatural life we can have in Christ and replace it with mediocrity, defeat, and insignificance. His name is Satan; he is the architect of the world system, the great deceiver, and the enemy of God and His people.

Satan is determined to destroy us and every vestige of Christ's kingdom. Peter warns us, "Be careful! Watch out for attacks from the Devil, your great enemy. He prowls around like a roaring lion, looking for some victim to devour" (1 Peter 5:8). But Satan is a defeated foe. Scripture proclaims, "The reason the Son of God appeared was to destroy the devil's work" (1 John 3:8, NIV). When Christ died and rose from the dead, Satan's power over us was completely destroyed.

Consider the following analogy:

The bite of a cobra is deadly, but scientists have developed an antidote. First, venom is drawn from the snake and injected into the bloodstream of a Belgian stallion. This mighty horse becomes deathly ill, but does not die because the antibodies in its blood are stronger than the cobra's poison. Then the horse's blood is used to make an antitoxin serum, which, when injected into the bloodstream of a cobra's victim, can save the person's life. In this way, the blood of the mighty stallion overcomes the power of the venom and preserves numerous lives.[1]

Jesus spilled His precious blood on the cross to defeat the "ancient serpent" and his poison of sin and death. The writer of Hebrews explains, "[Jesus] too shared in their humanity so that by His death He might destroy him who holds the power of death—that is, the devil" (2:14, NIV).

Satan appears to be so powerful. He controls the world system. He is the author of pornography, abortion, and all evils contrary to the Word of God. Often, we gape in awe and tremble at his power. But he is a roaring lion who has been defanged. Thanks to Christ, he is a defeated enemy, doomed to eternal destruction.

Satan knows he has been defeated, and that is why, like a cornered animal, he lashes out at those who are devoted to Christ. Since he cannot attack God directly, he hopes to harm those Christ saved and loves.

Satan frantically plots to undermine our relationship with God. He devises schemes to make us doubt our new identity and sabotage our supernatural life in Christ. He ensnares us in the daily worries and distractions of life, enticing us to neglect the study of God's Word, to forgo Spiritual Breathing, and to forsake fellowship with other believers. He fills us with pride until we are deaf and blind to the sin in our lives. He stirs up bitterness between us and fellow Christians to rob us of the wonderful peace intended for God's family. And he whispers lies into our minds so we distrust our heavenly Father's flawless character.

We have been given a free will to choose the way of God or the way of Satan, so Satan works hard to deceive us. In the Garden of Eden, Eve heard the deceptive words of Satan, then chose to believe them and eat the forbidden fruit. Satan will tempt us, but we are not defenseless. God has equipped us to resist any temptation (1 Corinthians 10:13). Paul admonishes Christians, "Be strong with the Lord's mighty power. Put on all of God's armor so that you will be able to stand firm against all strategies and tricks of the Devil" (Ephesians 6:10,11).

Our Spiritual War

We are at war, a war far more serious than any ever fought. This war has eternal consequences.

But regardless of Satan's strategies, we can stand firm. We can do this not because of our own goodness or might, but by relying on the strength of our supreme Savior. Christ frees us through His Word by revealing to us our identity in Him. He equips us for spiritual battle by clothing us in Himself and becoming our spiritual armor.

A unique member of God's amazing creation illustrates this point well. The "Moses sole" is a small, innocent-looking flatfish that thrives around the Red Sea. Named by Israelis, this fish resembles an ordinary flounder or sole, but contains a life-preserving defense against one of the deadliest life forms on earth: the great white shark. This fierce predator evokes terror in humans and inhabitants of the sea because of its ability to rip to pieces any foe —any foe, that is, except the Moses sole.

Our glorious Savior wants us to live a supernatural life of victory over Satan and his schemes.

Researchers discovered that the giant of the sea was powerless against this small flounder. The shark slices through the water toward the helpless fish, his mighty jaws wide open and his razor-sharp teeth glistening, but his jaws never close. Instead, the stunned predator hurries away, his jaws frozen open, while the delicate Moses sole contentedly swims around as though nothing had happened. The researchers learned that the Moses sole secretes a poison from glands along its fins. This milky poison is lethally toxic and envelops the gentle fish with a halo of protection.[2]

What a beautiful picture of the protection we can have against our deadly predator Satan, thanks to Christ. Because we are covered with the blood of Jesus, Satan cannot devour us. The Bible proclaims, "The one who is in you is greater than the one who is in the world" (1 John 4:4, NIV).

Our Effective Armor

Our glorious Savior wants us to live a supernatural life of victory over Satan and his schemes. Scripture explains the protection Christ offers by comparing it to a Roman soldier's armor:

> *Use every piece of God's armor to resist the enemy in the time of evil, so that after the battle you will still be standing firm. Stand your ground, putting on the sturdy belt of truth and the body armor of God's righteousness. For shoes, put on the peace that comes from the Good News, so that you will be fully prepared. In*

every battle you will need faith as your shield to stop the fiery arrows aimed at you by Satan. Put on salvation as your helmet, and take the sword of the Spirit, which is the word of God (Ephesians 6:13–17).

A Roman soldier's belt was essential. The soldier tucked the loose parts of his tunic under his belt so he could move freely without getting tangled in his clothes. The belt also kept his breastplate in place and held the scabbard for his sword.

Similarly, the belt of truth keeps our perception of reality securely bound to God's absolute truth. Satan's tactic is to deceive us with lies and distortions. But if we hold firmly to God's truth, we will have an accurate understanding of our spiritual identity and the magnificent character of our wonderful God. The belt of truth will keep us from getting tripped up by Satan's deceptions.

The Roman breastplate or body armor covered the torso from the neck to the thighs. It was intended to protect the heart and other vital organs. In a similar way, the breastplate of righteousness protects our spiritual self-image. Satan's scheme is to berate us with accusations and condemnation. But Christ has imparted His righteousness to us so we can enjoy an open and guilt-free relationship with our heavenly Father. And righteous living guards our deepest emotions and protects us from the mortal wounds caused by disobeying God.

A Roman soldier's boots gave him necessary traction and protection from the rugged terrain, enabling the soldier's freedom of movement.

Likewise, the shoes of peace promote freedom of movement and unity in the body of Christ. Satan wants to alienate us from God through disobedience, bitterness, and unforgiveness, for we are vulnerable when we are isolated from God and fellow believers. But when we allow peace to reign in our hearts and lives, we move closer to God and others. The shoes of peace equip us to dodge Satan's arrows of dissension and bitterness so we can stand in unity.

The Roman shield was almost as big as a refrigerator door. A line of soldiers bearing shields formed a wall of protection against the flaming arrows of the enemy.

Similarly, the shield of faith protects us against Satan's assaults. Satan bombards us with troubles and temptations. He entices us with worldly pleasures so we will distrust God's Word, doubt God's character, and dispute God's motives. Satan knows that the more we question God's commitment to us, the more we will depend upon ourselves. As we do, our shield is lowered, and we expose ourselves to Satan's wrath. But when we hold fast to our faith in God and join forces with our fellow believers, we are safe. For the shields Christ has provided for the church form a wall of protection against Satan's fury.

The Roman helmet protected soldiers from enemy cavalrymen taking aim at their heads with a three- to four-foot-long double-edged sword. The head is a strategic target because it gives direction to the rest of the body.

We can use God's inspired Word to attack strongholds of deception and drive Satan away.

The helmet of salvation protects us against Satan's efforts to attack our mind with poisonous thoughts. Standing firm in the knowledge of our salvation gives us the needed hope, confidence, and assurance to withstand Satan's propaganda. It wards off his efforts to provoke worry, fear, and discouragement, which can paralyze our Christian walk.

In addition, the helmet of salvation deflects any thoughts of despair with the hope of future glory. That is one reason Paul writes:

Always be full of joy in the Lord. I say it again—rejoice!...Remember, the Lord is coming soon. Don't worry about anything; instead, pray about everything. Tell God what you need, and thank Him for all He has done. If you do this, you will experience God's peace, which is far more wonderful than the human mind can understand. His peace will guard your hearts and minds as you live in Christ Jesus (Philippians 4:4–7).

Spiritual battles often begin in our minds. That is why it is essential for us to "put on salvation as our helmet."

Our Mighty Sword

The only offensive weapon Paul lists as part of our spiritual armor is the sword of the Spirit, which is the Word of God. The emphasis in this passage is on its use as an instrument like the Roman sword, a weapon that required skill and precision. If we know and understand God's Word, the Holy Spirit can guide us to use specific passages against Satan in each situation. Empowered by the Spirit, we can use God's inspired Word to attack strongholds of deception and drive Satan away.

David wrote, "I have hidden Your word in my

heart, that I might not sin against You" (Psalm 119:11). When Jesus was tempted by Satan in the wilderness, He quoted the Word of God. If we memorize Scripture, we too can hurl the truth of God's Word at Satan in times of temptation.

The following are promises you may want to commit to memory:

> *If you make the LORD your refuge, if you make the Most High your shelter, no evil will conquer you; no plague will come near your dwelling (Psalm 91:9,10).*

> *Remember that the temptations that come into your life are no different from what others experience. And God is faithful. He will keep the temptation from becoming so strong that you can't stand up against it. When you are tempted, He will show you a way out so that you will not give in to it (1 Corinthians 10:13).*

> *God blesses the people who patiently endure testing. Afterward they will receive the crown of life that God has promised to those who love Him (James 1:12).*

As you read God's Word, identify strategic passages to memorize that you can add to your arsenal of ammunition against Satan.

God's Mighty Power

Satan is an intimidating foe so we should take him and his schemes very seriously. However, our awesome God is infinitely more powerful. When we rely on Him, we can be assured of victory. Scripture promises, "Humble yourselves before God. Resist the Devil, and he will flee from you" (James 4:7). Satan has strongholds in this world, but miraculous things happen when Christians band together in the power of the Holy Spirit.

In Cali, Columbia, the lucrative business of illegal drugs was destroying the town, which was filled with terror because of the seven drug cartels that controlled the city. Hit men would kill anyone standing in the way of the drug kingpins.

A local pastor, Julio Ruibal, a beloved personal friend of mine, wanted to mobilize churches to pray against this stronghold of Satan. But the pastors in Cali were intimidated by their enemies.

After much fasting and prayer over the situation, Pastor Ruibal spoke openly and powerfully against the drug cartels. As a result, he received many death threats. Shortly after making his stand for what was right, Pastor Ruibal was shot and killed. At his memorial service, his wife described how her husband had lived under constant threat and how the enemy had tried to intimidate him in many ways. She then explained his great desire for the churches in Cali to be unified in the battle between Christ's kingdom and Satan's.

Hearing of Pastor Ruibal's example, the pastors were convicted of their failure to speak out and formed a covenant with each other. God led them to hold an all-night prayer rally in the city's stadium attended by tens of thousands of people.

God began to do incredible things in Cali. Within nine months, six out of the seven drug lords were arrested and the power of the drug cartels was broken.[3]

Our Lord and Savior is more powerful than any stronghold of Satan. To put on the armor of God is to put on Christ, who bought our salvation with His blood. He is our Deliverer from the evil one. To experience the reality of our deliverance, we must understand God's character and who we are in Him. Then, by faith, we can live in accordance with who we are in Christ.

Paul's Supernatural Race

Paul knew all about living a supernatural life in the midst of spiritual battle. He understood that the only way to be victorious is to first be crucified with Christ. He lived the words of Galatians 2:20, "I have been crucified with Christ and I no longer live, but Christ lives in me. The life I live in the body, I live by faith in the Son of God, who loved me and gave Himself for me" (NIV).

Not only did Paul surrender himself and all that he had to God, he even gave his life for the cause of Christ. After Paul had faithfully served his Lord and Savior for more than three decades, the Roman Emperor Nero ordered his execution by beheading. Some may question why God allowed this valiant, devoted servant to die such a tragic death. But the blood of the martyrs is precious to the Lord (Psalm 116:15). We have only once to live and once to die, and what better way to die than for the sake of our wonderful Savior and His eternal kingdom? Truly, Paul understood the truth of Jesus' words, "Whoever finds his life will lose it, and whoever loses his life for My sake will find it" (Matthew 10:39, NIV).

Years ago when I knelt in the dungeon in Rome where Paul awaited his execution, I wondered what it would be like to have listened in on his thoughts in those last hours before his death.

Can you picture Paul as he sits in that dreary dungeon? His face is weathered from the harsh winds of sea voyages and the intense sun of his many missionary journeys. Lines and furrows underscore the great strength of character mirrored in his expression. His eyes blaze with purpose, yet reveal an eternal depth of peace. They reflect a clear conscience and shine with the joy of his fellowship with Christ.

As he stands, we see that his body is battered, scarred from lashings, beatings, shipwrecks, and even a stoning. His back is bent from years of hard labor and from giving himself wholeheartedly for the church to the glory of Christ. But the spiritual muscles rippling beneath the wrinkled skin are stronger than ever. For him, to live has been Christ and to die will be gain. He runs all the faster in his race to live wholeheartedly for God now that he sees the finish line before him.

And what of his armor? It has stood the test of time and every assault of the evil one. His helmet of salvation has been dented, but not pierced. His belt of truth, stained with perspiration and blood, fits him more securely than ever. His breastplate of righteousness, battered by enemy fire, has remained intact. His boots of peace are well worn from the many miles he has traveled since he first met Christ. Yet in this last lap of his dedicated journey with his mighty Savior, their traction and protection make his steps sure. His shield of faith has not failed him these many years. The myriad burn marks and embedded broken shafts in the shield bear witness to its steadfast service in battle.

But it is Paul's sword of the Spirit that stuns his foes. Sharpened to a razor edge, it glistens like the sun and slices like a laser. Paul is skilled in wielding it. In these last hours, that sword is never out of Paul's hand. Even while chained between two centurion guards from Caesar's palace, he continues to preach the gospel. And though the guards are rotated every two hours to avoid being converted to Christ, many believe and take the life-transforming message of God's love and forgiveness back to Caesar's household.[4]

Now the soldiers come for him. He walks with them to his execution. He looks back, not at the great city of Rome, but at his life. He has no regrets—only joy at the countless people he has introduced to his Savior. His life has been an unimaginable adventure. Despite untold hardships, he would not trade one moment as a follower of Christ for years of wealth, notoriety, or ease. He rejoices that he has shared Christ's suffering, for he knows he will now share His glory. He has learned to be content in all things—even death.

A soldier raises a sword above him. Paul does not see it. He sees the finish line. He has run the good race. He has fought the good fight.

As his head falls from his body, his soul crosses the finish line into eternity. His race now finished, Paul hears those glorious words, "Well done, good and faithful servant."

We Are God's Priceless Masterpieces

Paul writes to the Ephesians, "We are God's masterpiece. He has created us anew in Christ Jesus, so that we can do the good things He planned for us long ago" (2:10). Like Paul, we, too, are God's priceless masterpiece, which He is carefully weaving into the image of Christ.

Each of us is a new creation in Christ with a wonderful new identity. We have God's Spirit within us to help us think, speak, and behave as we should. And we have a marvelous destiny both now and for eternity. Our Lord said, "I have come that they may have life, and have it to the full" (John 10:10, NIV). God assures us, "I know the plans I have for you. They are plans for good and not for disaster, to give you a future and a hope" (Jeremiah 29:11).

Before you were even born, before you placed your life into the hands of your wonderful Savior, God carefully designed a supernatural plan for you. He equipped you with a unique personality and special abilities to accomplish His purpose for your life to further His eternal kingdom. Wherever you go and whatever you do, you are Christ's ambassador. God wants you to introduce many others to your Savior and King.

Christ came to this world for one purpose—to seek and to save the lost (Luke 19:10). He said, "Come, follow me, and I will make you fishers of men" (Matthew 4:19, NIV). Everything else pales in comparison. Your walk with Christ involves

What spiritual legacy will you leave to your loved ones? Will they see your walk as worthy?

faithfully sharing with others the message of our Lord and Savior as a way of life. Invite Christ to live His life in and through you. Then you will experience a rich, full, and abundant life filled with divine purpose, deep meaning, eternal significance, and supernatural fruitfulness.

What spiritual legacy will you leave to your loved ones? Will they see your walk as worthy? Your feet standing firm on God's truth? Will your battered body reflect the beauty of God's character? Will you, like Paul, be an inspiring masterpiece in the gallery of people's hearts, attracting others to the One who died for you?

You have embarked on an incredible adventure. You do not know what awaits you around the next bend in life's journey. You cannot anticipate what dangers, hardships, or trials you may face. But you do know the One who walks with you. He is all-powerful, He is faithful, and He is worthy of your praise, trust, and total devotion. And He is always with you (Hebrews 13:5).

Place your hand in the hand of Jesus and, like the apostle Paul, walk with Him down the road of life. Your life here on earth may have its ups and downs, but as you deepen your relationship with God, you too will experience the supernatural, abundant life available only in Christ.

END NOTES

Chapter 1: Understanding Your Spiritual Blessings

1. Leslie Flynn, *Sermons Illustrated* (Holland, OH: November/December 1988).

2. "Theology News and Notes, October 1976," *Multnomah Message*, Spring 1993, p.1.

3. David Judge and Helmut Teichert, *Discovering God's Best: Right Thinking for Supernatural Living* (Sun River, MT: Turning Point Productions, 1994), Lesson 10.

4. Linda Seger, *The Art of Adaptation* (New York: Holt, 1992), p. 2.

5. "Entry," *Parables, Etc.* (Platteville, CO: Saratoga Press), December 1986.

6. "The One Who Would Die," *The Pastor's Story File* (Platteville, CO: Saratoga Press), March 1992.

Chapter 2: Allowing Christ to Live Through You

1. Alice Gray, "Dime Store Pearls," *Pulpit Helps*, June 1999, p. 6.

2. Elisabeth Eliot, *Shadow of the Almighty* (San Francisco: Harper & Row, 1956), p. 247.

3. *Sermons Illustrated* (Holland, OH: 1987).

4. Dr. Ralph Sockman, *Today in the Word* (Chicago, IL: Moody Bible Institute), October 1990, p. 14.

5. Donald Grey Barnhouse, *The Invisible War* (Grand Rapids, MI: Zondervan, 1965), p. 41.

6. Bruce Larson, *Believe and Belong* (Old Tappan, NJ: Power Books, 1982).

Chapter 3: Thriving in God's Spiritual Family

1. Charles Colson and Ellen Santilli Vaughn, *Against the Night: Living in the New Dark Ages* (Ann Arbor, MI: Servant Publications, 1999), p. 98.

2. Lewis Timberlake, "Interdependence," www.sermonillustrations.com/interdependence.htm.

3. David Judge and Helmut Teichert, *Discovering God's Best: Right Thinking for Supernatural Living* (Sun River, MT: Turning Point Productions, 1994), Lesson 14.

4. Jack Kyrtle, "Ford Encouraged by Edison," *Encyclopedia of 7,700 Illustrations*, *Signs of the Times*, Ed. Paul Lee Tan, Th. D., (Hong Kong: Nordica International Ltd., 1996), pp. 338, 339.

5. Calvin Hunt, February 1998 interview by John Barber, *WorldChangers* radio (Orlando, FL: Campus Crusade for Christ).

6. "Bringing in the New," *The Pastor's Story File* (Platteville, CO: Saratoga Press), June 1992.

Chapter 4: Experiencing Supernatural Power

1. Steve Blankenship, "Power," www.bible.org/p-q/p-q-77.htm.

2. Lyle W. Dorsett, "Ministry Maverick," *Moody Magazine Online*, www.moodypress.org/MOODYMAG/maverick.htm.

3. Robert A. Morey, *Battle of the Gods: The Gathering Storm in Modern Evangelicalism* (Southbridge, MA: Crown Publications, 1989), p. 36.

Chapter 5: Achieving Triumph Over Adversity

1. Joni Eareckson Tada, *Her Story* (New York: Inspirational Press, 1994).

2. Thomas Watson, *All Things for Good,* reprint of 1663 original (Edinburgh, UK: The Banner of Truth Trust).

3. *Leadership Magazine,* Vol. 4, No. 1, p. 83.

4. Jack Canfield and Mark Victor Hansen, eds., *Chicken Soup for the Soul* (Deerfield Beach, FL: Health Communications, Inc. 1993), p. 65.

5. *Today in the Word* (Chicago, IL: Moody Bible Institute), June 11, 1989.

6. Winston Churchill, first speech as Prime Minister to the House of Commons, May 13, 1940, London, England, www.winstonchurchill.org/blood.htm.

7. Halford E. Luccock, *Unfinished Business: Short Diversions on Religious Themes* (New York: Harper, 1956).

Chapter 6: Possessing Infinite Joy

1. "The Bible Friend," *Turning Point Magazine* (San Diego: Turning Point), May 1993.

2. Philip Comfort, Ph. D., ed. *Life Application Bible Commentary: Philippians, Colossians, Philemon* (Wheaton, IL: Tyndale House, 1995), p. 25.

3. C. S. Lewis, *The Weight of Glory* (New York: Collier Books, 1980), p. 4.

4. C. Neil Strait, "Do You Know," *Parables, Etc.* (Platteville, CO; Saratoga Press), August 1990.

5. David L. McKenna, *MegaTruth: The Church in the Age of Information* (San Bernardino, CA: Here's Life Publishers, 1986).

6. *Today in the Word* (Chicago, IL: Moody Bible Institute), June 1988, p. 18.

Chapter 7: Standing Victoriously in Christ

1. Ralph W. Harris, *Enrichment Magazine: Journal for Pentecostal Ministry* (Springfield, MO: Gospel Publishing House), Summer 1996.

2. "God is Greater," *The Pastor's Story File* (Platteville, CO: Saratoga Press), April 1995.

3. *Transformations: A Documentary*, produced by Global Net Productions (The Sentinel Group, 1999).

4. Adapted from R. Kent Hughes, *Ephesians: The Mystery of the Body of Christ* (Wheaton, IL: Crossway Books, 1990), pp. 254, 255.

William R. Bright

Founder, Chairman, and President Emeritus,
Campus Crusade for Christ International

From a small beginning in 1951, the organization he began now has a presence in 196 countries in areas representing 99.6% of the world's population. Campus Crusade for Christ has more than 70 ministries and major projects, utilizing more than 25,000 full-time and 500,000 trained volunteer staff. Each ministry is designed to help fulfill the Great Commission, Christ's command to help carry the gospel of God's love and forgiveness in Christ to every person on earth.

Born in Coweta, Oklahoma, on October 19, 1921, Bright graduated with honors from Northeastern State University, and completed five years of graduate study at Princeton and Fuller Theological Seminaries. He holds five honorary doctorates from prestigious institutions and has received numerous other recognitions, including the ECPA Gold Medallion Lifetime Achievement Award (2001), the Golden Angel Award as International Churchman of the Year (1982), and the $1.1 million Templeton Prize for Progress in Religion (1996), which he dedicated to promoting fasting and prayer throughout the world.

He has received the first-ever Lifetime Achievement Award from his alma mater (2001).

Bright has authored more than 100 books, booklets, videos and audio tapes, as well as thousands of articles and pamphlets, some of which have been printed in most major languages and distributed by the millions. Among his books are: *Come Help Change the World, The Secret, The Holy Spirit, A Man Without Equal, A Life Without Equal, The Coming Revival, The Transforming Power of Fasting & Prayer, Red Sky in the Morning* (co-author), *GOD: Discover His Character, Living Supernaturally in Christ,* and the booklet *Have You Heard of the Four Spiritual Laws?* (which has an estimated 2.5 billion circulation).

He has also been responsible for many individual initiatives in ministry, particularly in evangelism. For example, the *JESUS* film, which he conceived and financed through Campus Crusade, has, by latest estimates, been viewed by over 4.6 billion people in 236 nations and provinces.

Bright and his wife, Vonette, who assisted him in founding Campus Crusade for Christ, live in Orlando, Florida. Their two sons, Zac and Brad, and their wives, Terry and Katherine, are also in full-time Christian ministry.